"I don't ever plan to remarry."

He didn't have to make up this whole story for her. So they weren't a match in the love department. The idea that Graham would never remarry was crazy.

"You don't have to explain anything to me. It's not like we were on a date."

"I know. But I'm telling you, I wouldn't be anyway. I'm really never getting remarried."

Graham definitely seemed the type to marry and grow old with someone. Lucy could picture him having more kids, finding a stepmom for Mattie. The girl would love it. Maybe having a mom again would take away some of Mattie's serious nature and let her be a kid.

What would keep Graham from considering marriage again?

"Was your marriage…that bad?" Graham's frown told her what she already knew—she shouldn't have asked.

"No. It was that good."

Ouch. Why did those words sting? She hardly knew this man. She'd been in town two weeks, and yet his response made her feel as if she'd been shoved from a moving car.

This had nothing to do with her. Then why did it feel as though it did?

Jill Lynn is a member of the American Christian Fiction Writers group and won the ACFW Genesis award in 2013. She has a bachelor's degree in communications from Bethel University. A native of Minnesota, Jill now lives in Colorado with her husband and two children. She's an avid reader of happily-ever-afters and a fan of grace, laughter and thrift stores. Connect with her at jill-lynn.com.

Books by Jill Lynn

Love Inspired

Falling for Texas
Her Texas Family

Her Texas Family

Jill Lynn

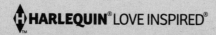

HARLEQUIN® LOVE INSPIRED®

Recycling programs
for this product may
not exist in your area.

LOVE INSPIRED BOOKS

ISBN-13: 978-0-373-71956-3

Her Texas Family

Copyright © 2016 by Jill Buteyn

www.Harlequin.com

Printed in U.S.A.

I praise You because I am fearfully and wonderfully made; Your works are wonderful, I know that full well.
—*Psalms* 139:14

To my husband: God blessed me big when He gave me you. Thank you for being better than I could have ever imagined, for making me laugh and for always cleaning my mess of a car. I love you!

Chapter One

Climbing a tree in heels? Not one of her better decisions.

Lucy Grayson held her cell phone toward the Texas sky and prayed for reception. The prayer didn't work, nor did her ascent, which she'd hoped would somehow get her closer to a cell tower. Just beyond the tree, Lucy's pitiful car sat on the side of the road with a flat tire, stranded like a woman with a broken high heel.

Her whole life was packed into that car…all of her shoes, most of her clothes and everything else she could cram in. Which made the thought of clearing out her trunk in order to reach her spare tire daunting. And so not necessary. Not if she could get hold of her sister and brother-in-law and borrow their truck, loading everything into it instead of dumping her things on the side of the road.

She was mere miles from their home, so she *could* walk. But surely her phone was just being ornery. It had to have some reception. Another impatient glance at the screen told her nothing had changed in the past twenty seconds of her life.

Drat.

Lucy wiggled her left foot, attempting to free it from her red ankle bootee without reaching down to untie it. She certainly couldn't climb down in these shoes. She'd slipped a few times on the way up and didn't want to risk the same during her descent.

A look down had her stomach tripping all over itself. Lucy had climbed higher than she realized, hoping just a little more height would give her the results she wanted.

Averting her gaze to the limb directly in front of her, she shimmied out of her left ankle boot. It dropped to the ditch below with a muted thud. The sole of her bare foot met rough bark, and she started the same process with her other shoe. One final kick of her heel against the tree limb sent it flying from her foot. Perfect. Now to get down.

A yelp sounded.

At the bottom of the tree, a man stood staring up at her, his hand pressed against his forehead. Oh, no. She hadn't…

"Is there another shoe coming that I need to be aware of?"

Lucy pressed her lips together to hold back the ill-timed amusement that begged for release. Keeping her right arm wrapped around the tree trunk, she pointed to her other shoe, which had landed a few feet away from him. "No. Sorry about that."

"It's okay. I think." He stopped rubbing his forehead, leaving the red mark from her boot weapon visible. "What are you doing up there?"

Now, *that* was a tough question to answer. Picnicking? Going for a climb? Moving to Texas? Nothing seemed quite right. And her actual answer, now that she had an audience, did sound a bit…unusual. Or for her, usual. Her family would definitely call this a typical Lucy moment.

"I was making a phone call." Or trying to.

The man's brow crinkled, and he continued to peer up at her with confusion. Lucy scrambled down the tree, each bough swaying under her now bare feet. Despite feeling somewhat like a monkey, the sensation of being free did give her a thrill.

She landed in front of him with a very ungraceful, un-dancer-like crash.

During her descent, he'd crossed his arms over a white-checked oxford he wore with crisp jeans and brown leather shoes that even her fashion sense approved of. He was a head taller than her, with chocolate hair and midnight-green eyes.

A wave of recognition rushed through her, causing her skin to prickle with awareness.

Lucy remembered this man from her sister's wedding. She didn't know his name. She just recalled seeing him that night.

At Olivia and Cash's reception, he'd been dancing with a little girl. The small child had worn glasses and a frilly dress, and her shoes had been propped up on his toes as they'd twirled around the dance floor. Lucy had melted at the sight. After all, she was a dancer.

Right. That was what had attracted her attention. Not the fact that the guy was totally droolworthy and hadn't noticed her for a second. Usually when guys tried to gain her attention, she couldn't care less. This one hadn't known she existed…although now that she'd clocked him in the head with a shoe, she'd be unforgettable. For all the wrong reasons.

Did it really matter that he was looking at her without an ounce of recognition?

It wasn't as if Lucy wanted to follow her sister's path and sign up for a wedding ring while in Texas. She didn't do serious relationships. She did fun. Lucy had made the decision way back in high school, and she'd stuck to it ever since. It had taken only one experience—one moment of going gooey over a guy—to teach her she much preferred to keep things light. And it was a lesson that had served her well over the years.

"I saw your flat tire and thought you might need help." The look of bewilderment still etched across his face had her fighting a smile. Not everyone knew what to make of her personality. But did he have to look *so* shocked? So he'd found her up a tree trying to make a phone call. She wasn't acting *that* crazy. "Where are you headed?"

"I'm actually moving here. Right now I'm trying to get to my sister's house, which is just—" North? East? Lucy searched for the Rocky Mountains that had declared which way was west for the whole of her life, but was only met with the low green hills that permeated Texas Hill Country. Finally, she just pointed. "That direction."

He reached forward and removed something from her hair, tossing it to the side. Looked like a baby branch by the size of the thing. How had she not noticed that monstrosity hitchhiking a ride on the way down?

"Your sister?"

"Yeah. Olivia Maddox." Even after seven months of her sister being married, that new last name still felt so weird to say.

"Graham Redmond." He offered his hand, and Lucy shook it, introducing herself. "Cash is a friend of mine."

Lucy just nodded. *I know. Men.* This conversation only served to support her philosophy of keeping them in the fun/friend category instead of getting overly involved with one.

"So, are you moving to Texas for work?"

"For fun." For the most part. Lucy could also mention that she couldn't get along with her previous employer and that the move had been perfect timing for getting away from a certain guy, but she didn't feel like delving into those things now. Or maybe ever. "And partly for work. I have a part-time job lined up teaching dance." Although teaching one measly dance class wasn't enough to pay her bills. Lucy's first priority in town was to find a job that did. Scratch that. Her first priority was to get to her sister's house. The second would be to make sure she could pay for rent and groceries.

But at least she knew she was doing the right thing in moving. After the trouble with her old boss, she'd prayed for an out. Olivia had called about the dance-instructor opening a few days later. Moving to Texas had been an answer to prayer and just the kind of adventure Lucy craved.

She reached out and gently touched the mark on his head. "I'm sorry about hitting you with my shoe. Does it hurt?"

He flinched as if her hand inflicted more pain than her boot had. "It's fine."

"But it looks so red." A perfect match for the color of her shoe. And it was forming a rather large bump. "How do you know? Maybe you should get it checked out."

"I'm a doctor." He tenderly touched the spot. "I'm not worried about it."

"Okay." She shrugged. Why did she care so much? Sure, her shoe had caused the welt, but he obviously didn't want her interference. Fine by her.

She could say the same back to him. Since he'd so nobly stopped to help her, she would reassure him she didn't need his assistance. He could keep heading wherever he'd been heading, and she'd figure out how to get to her sister's or change the tire on her own.

Graham Redmond didn't need to fill the role of dashing hero in her life. Because, as the residents of Fredericksburg would soon find out, Lucy wasn't a damsel in distress who needed to be rescued.

She could rescue herself.

Usually people worried about pulling over to help with a stranded vehicle because a dangerous person could be planning some kind of highway robbery...not because they feared shoes falling from the sky and almost knocking them out cold.

The place where Graham's forehead had been introduced to a high heel still smarted, but he ignored the throbbing in order to figure out the woman in front of him. She seemed…young. Flighty. And not just because she'd been up a tree when he'd pulled over at the sight of her stranded Volkswagen Beetle. She twisted long, blond curls over one shoulder as she bent to pick up her shoes, sliding them back on her feet and then tying the small black laces. Skinny jeans met with a blue-and-white-checked shirt extending from under a navy sweater. How old could she be? Early twenties? She acted a bit like a teenager, though her looks didn't support that theory.

And neither did the math. If Graham remembered correctly, Olivia's sister was just a few years younger than she was.

He pointed up the tree she'd just climbed down like some kind of gymnast. "Did you say you were making a phone call?"

"Yeah."

"If you were calling for help, I can change the tire for you."

She huffed, crossing her arms. Had he said something offensive?

"I know how to change a tire. At least, I'm sure I could figure it out," she said, voice quieter. "There's probably instructions. How hard can it be?" She motioned to her car. "I was calling my brother-in-law because my car's packed full. Every inch of it. I'd have to unpack the back to get to my spare, and since I'm almost to my sister's house, it made more sense to see if they could bring the truck. That way I could load everything into it, and I wouldn't have to move all of my stuff onto the side of the road."

Her convoluted logic made sense. Graham must be losing his mind.

"So, you need a ride to Cash and Olivia's? That I can do."

Her eyes narrowed to slits. "Were you…headed in that direction?"

"No, but it's not far."

The toe of her boot tapped as she contemplated. A quick shake of her head was coupled with tight-pressed lips. "No, thank you."

No? What did she plan to do? Walk? Hope for cell reception? She was crazy to think he'd leave without helping her.

"I don't want to interrupt your plans."

What plans? Graham hadn't done anything social in the past…five years or so. Not since Mattie was born and then losing Brooke. He didn't exactly have a busy social life. Work? He had plenty of that. And colored pictures on his fridge. He had lots of those. Plus, he played a mean game of Go Fish on Saturday nights.

"My daughter and I were just headed home. It will only take us a few minutes to drop you off." If he had to be direct or demanding in order for her to accept his help, so be it. Anything to make this encounter go a bit faster. Lucy made him feel…uncomfortable. As if he wanted to loosen his tie, even though he wasn't wearing one today.

After a minute of contemplation, she let out an earth-shaking sigh. "Fine." The word came through gritted teeth. "I appreciate your help."

He got the impression she didn't like his offer of help one bit, especially when her forced tone was accompanied by crossed arms and eyes that flashed with displeasure. Their bright blue color punched him in the chest. Unique. Brilliant. He wasn't sure exactly how to describe them. Not that he needed to write a report. What he needed to do was drop this woman off at her sister's and then head home to get his week organized before the craziness of Monday hit. No doubt his medical office would be slammed tomorrow morning as it was almost every Monday. But at least there he felt useful. At least there he was too busy for the images of his past failures to haunt him.

"Let me grab my purse."

While Lucy did that, Graham opened the trunk to his car and checked the bolt pattern on his spare. It didn't match the one on Lucy's wheels. Just as well. Graham wasn't sure he'd live through the experience of changing a flat tire with this woman. He'd seen what Lucy could do with a shoe. What harm could she accomplish with a lug wrench?

He started his BMW and pulled up parallel to her car. She came over with full hands, so he leaned across the seat and popped the passenger door open. Lucy slid in, dropping a purse and jacket on the floor of his car. When she shut the door, the scent of lime and coconut came with her.

It was the end of January, and she smelled like summer. Graham hadn't known the season had its own scent before.

He motioned to the backseat. "This is my daughter, Matilda Grace. Everyone calls her Mattie."

Lucy buckled and twisted to face the backseat while he put the car in Drive. "Hi, Mattie Grace. It's nice to meet you."

In the rearview mirror, Graham could see the name earned a smile from Mattie. A shy one.

"I'm Lucy."

"*Ms.* Lucy," he said.

Those eyes of hers jutted to him, giving off a spark of something close to annoyance before she softened and turned back to Mattie. "What grade are you in?"

"Kindergarten."

Graham could feel the mix of interest and shyness oozing from Mattie in the backseat. His daughter tended to be on the serious side with an older-than-her-years nature. She was compliant, sweet and entirely more than he deserved. He thanked God for her every day.

The short distance to Cash and Olivia's took only a few minutes. When they arrived, the three of them got out, making their way up the wide porch steps.

Lucy knocked, then opened the door, calling out her arrival. She stepped inside, and Olivia squealed, tugging her into a very enthusiastic hug.

Cash Maddox appeared at the door, surprise evident. "Hey, Red. Mattie. Come on in."

At thirty-one years old, Graham was a few years older than Cash, but the two of them had grown up together and they'd always had an easy friendship. Cash was one of the few people who understood losing someone—not that he'd lost a wife, like Graham had, but grief was one emotion they shared knowledge of.

Even though Graham was close to six feet tall, Cash towered over him. His friend passed him in inches…and brawn. The fact that Cash ran a ranch from dawn till dusk and Graham saw patients inside all day might have a little something to do with that second thing.

"I can't believe you're finally here!" Olivia took a step back from her sister, her brown hair contrasting with Lucy's sunshine blond. "Where have you been? I thought from the last time I talked to you that you were going to get here an hour ago."

"Flat tire." Lucy grimaced.

"Where's your car? Did you change it? What happened?"

Lucy laughed, a lyrical sound that tightened Graham's throat. Was he coming down with something? There'd been a lot of rash/fever combinations in the office last week. It was either that or this woman had some strange effect on him.

Definitely had to be germs.

"Still on the road. No, I didn't change it because I didn't want to unpack everything. And Graham stopped and ended up giving me a ride."

Olivia's gaze jumped to him. Seemed she hadn't noticed his arrival. But then, he would guess Lucy's entrance anywhere would pretty much overshadow anyone else's.

"Thanks for taking care of my little sister, Graham."

He nodded.

"Yeah." Lucy flashed bright white teeth in his direction. "Thanks for the ride."

He opened his mouth but no sound came out.

Olivia bent to eye level with Mattie while Graham still choked on his words. Or lack of them. Honestly. What was wrong with him?

"Hey, Mattie. It's good to see you." Her hand trailed along one of Mattie's brown pigtails, coaxing a grin from his daughter.

"Mattie is practically a superhero. She swooped in and saved me from having to make the choice between a long walk or unloading my car." Lucy shared a fist bump with Mattie, her head tilting in his direction. "Along with her trusty sidekick."

Graham's mouth gave in to a slight curve at the acknowledgment. He'd take the demoted status just for the look on his daughter's face.

Lucy turned to Cash. "About my car. I thought maybe I could borrow your truck. I'll change the tire. I can do everything if you'll just let me—"

"What?" Cash snorted. "You really think I'm going to send you back out to take care of a flat tire on your own? What kind of brother do you think I am? I'll take care of it."

By the way Lucy's chin jutted out, she wasn't satisfied with that answer. "I don't want you to have to deal with all of my stuff. The car's jammed full."

"I have a thing for taking care of little sisters, and since Rachel up and left for college, you're stuck with my overprotective nature. I might even have a spare out in the garage we could use. And if I don't, not that much can fit into that tin-can car of yours anyway."

"Listen, McCowboy." Her finger poked into Cash's gray T-shirt. "I'm absolutely helping with the tire. Don't even think about going without me."

McCowboy?

Cash shook his head, glancing at Olivia with amusement. "You did mention what a complex your sister has about accepting help."

So it wasn't just Graham she fought. Good to know.

Lucy squeaked. "That's not true! I just accepted a ride to your house." The woman beamed as if she should win a prize.

"Lucy's car is near the big oak tree that got hit by lightning when we were in high school." Graham's lips twitched, and Lucy's eyes started dancing with mischief. She certainly wasn't embarrassed about her tree climb. He got the impression not much caused her to experience that particular emotion.

"So, Graham." Olivia turned to him. "It's actually perfect that you picked up my sister. I wanted the two of you to meet."

A cold sweat snaked under his collar. Was Olivia trying to set him up with her flighty sister? *Not* going to happen. Graham had already had the love of his life. Now he had Mattie and absolutely no desire to remarry. Olivia would just have to take her matchmaking ideas elsewhere.

"Lulu, Graham's office manager is out on maternity leave and he needs someone to fill in."

What?

He hadn't expected that. And this conversation sounded like trouble. Yes, the woman who ran Graham's front office had gone on maternity leave unexpectedly early last week, leaving him completely strapped, but that didn't mean Lucy Grayson was the right person for the position.

"I think it would be a perfect start for you, Lulu." Olivia gave Graham a look he couldn't quite decipher. Did she expect him to offer Lucy a job right here and now? Bend down on one knee and start begging?

Lucy studied him long enough to make him squirm, determination sparking in her eyes. "I do have a business degree. I don't have experience in a medical office, but I could learn."

How was he going to get out of this? Graham wanted someone for the position who could walk right in and know what they were doing. Someone with experience. Exactly the type of person he'd been looking for since well before Hollie went into early labor. Unfortunately, after three different temps had filled in last week, Graham was beginning to think that person didn't exist.

Olivia was still talking about the possibility of Lucy working for him, how it would be a great fit, how it would be beneficial for both of them.

Graham could only stare. He felt as though he was sliding down a treacherous slope with little chance of rescue.

"Sorry, Red." Cash looked far too amused and not nearly concerned enough. "I don't think there's any saving you from this one."

"Seriously? You're just going to leave me hanging? I am never prescribing anything for you ever again."

Cash laughed. "I can't imagine anyone going up against Liv and coming away with a win. Trust me, I know from experience." His gaze slid to his wife, filled with enough admiration that a twinge of jealousy came over Graham.

Graham remembered that look, that feeling, well. He'd give anything to look at his wife like that again. But those days were gone, and he was healing. He was moving on. Just not into another relationship.

Unfortunately, at the moment, his friend was right. By the look on Olivia's face, she was going to win this battle. Graham wanted to run for the door. Either that or rewind the evening and not stop at the sight of a stranded yellow Beetle.

"What do you think? Should we give it a try?" Lucy looked so hopeful that something in him tugged. She couldn't be worse than the temps, could she? Maybe he was overreacting about the fact that he'd found her up a tree on the side of the road. Perhaps they could help each other out.

She'd have to be trained, but he'd figure out that part. Besides, it wasn't as if he had any other choices lined up.

Graham would usually pray about a decision like this. Take his time. Wait on God's guidance. But he was desperate. Desperate enough to hire a woman who looked like a model, smelled like sunshine and didn't have a lick of experience.

Her words came back to him. A try, she'd said.

The tension in his body untangled. That was what he would do. He'd hire her on a trial basis. That way, when she couldn't do the job, he'd have no issue letting her go.

Chapter Two

On Tuesday morning, Lucy sat behind a wide receptionist desk in Graham's medical office and stared at the blinking black beast in front of her. Some might call it a phone. Lucy deemed it an instrument of torture. It boasted a number on the small gray screen—one that kept growing as the number of people waiting for her to answer increased. When Graham's nurse, Danielle, had trained Lucy on it early this morning, she'd called it the queue. Lucy didn't have such a nice name for it.

It scared her more than spiders or spam.

On Sunday night, she and Graham had hammered out a few details. An agreement of sorts. They'd agreed to give working together a try. He'd put a lot of emphasis on that last word, and Lucy felt an underlying sense of tension that normally didn't invade her life. Graham probably thought she was completely unqualified for the position. And he'd be right. Which meant she needed to prove herself today.

She knew her opportunity to work for Graham had everything to do with God and Olivia making it happen and very little to do with her office skills—which were nonexistent.

On Monday, when Lucy had moved into her above-garage apartment in town—the one her sister had lived in last year—she'd scanned the paper for any other job openings she might be qualified for, just in case working for Graham didn't pan out.

There weren't any.

Since her move to Texas had come up quickly, Lucy hadn't had time to save. She didn't have any reserves for covering an extended period of time without work. And since she absolutely refused to ask her parents or Olivia and Cash for money, she needed this job.

How hard could it be? she'd thought. Answer a phone. File some charts. But after a few of the calls she'd already fielded this morning, Lucy was afraid to touch the flashing beast in front of her. Since timidity wasn't in her nature, she took a steadying breath and yanked the receiver up, pressing it to her ear.

"Dr. Redmond's office. May I help you?"

"This is Walt Birl. Who's this?"

Another favorite question of the morning. Who was she? What was she doing in town? And from two grandmothers— was she interested in meeting their grandsons?

"Lucy Grayson. I'm new to town. I'm running from some unsolved crimes in Colorado. What can I do for you, Mr. Birl?"

Stunned silence.

Lucy winced and looked at the phone as though she could see his reaction through the small black holes. Oops. Perhaps not her best move. Wasn't she planning to be professional today? Prove to Graham he hadn't made a mistake in hiring her?

When she put the phone back to her ear, loud cackling greeted her. "I like you. Listen, I have a rash I need to discuss with someone."

Don't pick me. Don't pick me.

"It's kind of round, though there's a few spots—"

"Mr. Birl, you really need to speak with the nurse or

schedule an appointment with Dr. Redmond. I'll be no help at all."

"Okay. Transfer me to Danielle, then."

Lucy sighed with relief, then pressed a few buttons on the phone, hoping the call actually went to Danielle's phone and voice mail in the back.

She dived into the waiting queue. It took her almost two hours to wade through the calls, partially since everyone had to get the lowdown on her before talking medical business. Finally, the screen didn't show anyone on hold. Lucy did a happy dance, chair sliding back and forth with her movements.

"What are you doing?"

She screeched. Graham had come down the hall during her happy dance...with a patient. Thankfully the frazzled mom with a toddler on her hip simply waved and walked out the front doors.

Lucy motioned to the phone. "Just celebrating getting through the phone calls."

"Oh." Graham sported the same look of confusion he'd been wearing when he'd stopped to help with her flat tire. "Okay." He shrugged and disappeared down the hall again. Even slightly snarly, the man still managed to look good. He also had impeccable taste in clothes. A crisp white button-down shirt and black dress pants. A tie that teased some of the lighter flecks of green from his eyes. He reminded Lucy of an actor on a television show she used to watch. Definitely Hollywood for this small town.

Digging into her purse, Lucy plucked out her phone and texted her sister.

What are you doing?

When it beeped a response, Lucy gave a silent cheer. Liv almost never responded to texts during the day because she was normally in the middle of teaching one of her French classes at the high school.

Between classes. How's the first day?

How to answer that?

Exciting.

Lol. Yeah, rt. R u still at work? Have u caused any trouble?

Lucy's lips curved. Her sister knew her too well.

Yes and no.

Though Lucy had simply meant to answer Liv's questions in order, the humor in it made her perk up. Let her sister wonder a bit at that.

Lucy?!!!??

She laughed and slid the phone back into her purse. It took her a few minutes to figure out how to print the updated appointment schedule so she could pull the patient charts for the rest of the day. Once she did, Lucy did a pirouette on her way to pick up the sheet from the printer located in the far left corner of the reception space. Now that the phone calls had slowed, she was doing okay. Maybe she'd get the hang of this job faster than she'd expected.

Graham walked into the reception space and dropped some charts on top of the pile on her desk that needed to be reshelved, then turned and scanned the files.

"Just grabbing my next appointment. I'm sure you haven't had time to pull anything with handling the phones this morning."

"Thanks." That was nice. Maybe the man didn't just speak in grunts all the time. Actually, she knew he didn't. She'd heard him being great with the patients. And she'd seen him interact with Mattie the other night. Graham looked at his daughter as if she made the sun rise and set each day. From what Lucy had gathered in the short time they'd been together on Sunday, she agreed with that assessment. Mattie was supercute with her red glasses, glossy hair and bright, inquisitive green eyes that seemed to quietly observe everything around her.

Seeing Graham act so sweet with Mattie had melted Lucy a bit.

But he certainly hadn't sprinkled any of that sugar in her direction. With Lucy, he kept a polite distance and only spoke caveman.

She considered the way Graham obviously adored Mattie to be his best quality. Second best? His choice in cologne.

Inhaling, she inched closer to his back as he faced the charts. Woodsy. Spicy. Definitely worth a second sniff. She leaned in just a bit more.

Graham grabbed a chart and turned, almost bumping into her. Lucy jumped back, not realizing how close she'd migrated in her efforts to breathe him in.

He stared at her, those dark, stormy eyes wide.

"Sorry." She took a step back. "I—" *Want to smell you?* Nope. Not first-day-on-the-job words.

Graham's brow furrowed. "You okay?"

"I'm great." *You just smell distractingly good. What kind of cologne is that? Would it be weird if I requested you wear it every day? Would it be even worse if I grabbed your perfectly knotted grass-green tie, tugged you forward and buried my nose along the collar of your shirt?*

Graham made his way past her, pausing by the edge of the desk. "We'll turn off the phones for lunch. I need to grab Mattie from school. She has a half day today. But

Danielle can answer any questions you have after you're done eating."

"Sounds good." Lucy pasted on a bright smile and waited until Graham disappeared down the hall before letting it fall from her face. Phew. That had been a close one.

She searched the shelves filled with rows and rows of manila folders reaching up to the ceiling behind her desk and along the wall. Looked as though the chart she needed was on the top row. She glanced around. Not a stool or chair to be found besides the rolling one behind her desk. At five and a half feet, Lucy wasn't necessarily short—unless she compared herself with her sister or father—but she was pretty sure she needed some assistance to reach the top row.

She rolled the office chair over, aligned it in front of the shelves, then dropped to the ground and locked the wheels into place. Lucy stood and put one foot on the chair, then changed her mind and unzipped her brown, high-heeled boots. She removed them from her feet, rather proud of herself for taking the time to ensure her safety. She'd learned her lesson about climbing in heels.

Her outfit for the day—an army-green dress that swished above the knee, cinched with a multicolored belt and accessorized with an assortment of mismatched beaded bracelets—wasn't exactly ideal for climbing on a chair. But Lucy would make it quick. She'd grab the chart and be back down before anyone knew what she'd been up to.

After giving the chair a test shove to make sure the wheels didn't roll, Lucy stepped up, toes digging into the leather. She heard the front door to the office open but kept her concentration on the charts. Scanning the names until she found the one she needed, she slid it from the shelf. The chair moved under her feet. She gasped and reached for the shelf, dropping the file in order to hang on with both hands. The grip stopped her movement. A shaky, relieved breath whooshed out, causing dust to fly off a few files in front of her. Another close one.

She jumped from the chair before it could cause further damage, bare feet landing on the floor with a thud.

Lucy found herself face-to-face with a young man who'd appeared behind the receptionist desk during her chart hunt. He screamed cowboy. Broad shoulders in a blue plaid shirt. Boots peeking out from jeans.

The skin around his brown eyes crinkled. "I apologize for being in your space, ma'am. When I walked in, I saw you wobbling on the chair and thought you might need a hand. Looked like you were about to take quite the tumble. And yet, here you stand."

He had a Southern drawl and he'd called her *ma'am*. Yee-haw. "I appreciate the backup."

"I'm the one who called to see if Doc Redmond could squeeze me in for this." His right shirtsleeve was rolled up, a nasty-looking gash visible. He situated the cloth he was holding to fully cover the wound. "I'm Hunter McDermott. My family's ranch edges your brother-in-law's."

She introduced herself, and dimples sprouted in his cheeks.

"The famous Lucy Grayson. Do you really think anyone in this town doesn't know who you are?"

At least one person hadn't.

"Sooo…" He stretched the word out. "I suppose you saw a bit of Rachel back in Colorado." Hunter's gaze flitted away before meeting hers again. "How's she doing?"

Oh. Now Lucy knew the lay of the land. Wonder if Rachel Maddox knew she'd left behind one interested cowboy in Texas when she'd headed to Colorado for college.

"Rachel's great. Busy with classes and off-season volleyball training. And not dating anyone that I know of."

Interest flashed on his face before he cleared his throat. "That's good, then. I mean, not that she's not dating anyone. Just that she's doing well. I—"

Hunter shrugged and shook his head, and Lucy's amusement and pity for the guy doubled. He grabbed the chart she'd dropped—amazingly the contents had stayed anchored inside—and handed it to her. "Here you go."

"Thanks." Lucy stepped toward the desk to set the file down and stumbled over her forgotten boots on the floor. Though she didn't *exactly* need it, Hunter reached out, grabbing her arms to steady her. They shared an amused grin.

"I'll let Dr. Redmond know you're here."

"No need." Graham spoke from behind Lucy, his curt tone zinging along her spine. "Come on back, Hunter."

Hunter nodded at Lucy, then stepped around to the front of the reception desk.

"I'll meet you in exam room two."

At that, the cowboy disappeared down the hallway, leaving Lucy with a disgruntled Graham.

Uh-oh. Why did he look so upset? Was it something she'd done? She could just imagine the long list of complaints Graham could have against her. After all, she'd literally been thrown into the job this morning with very little training. Lucy hadn't been taught much more than how to deal with the phone and a quick lesson on the appointment scheduling system. Had she mis-scheduled an appointment? Lost a chart? Offended a patient?

She didn't know the answer. She only knew by the tension tugging on Graham's mouth and the crease cutting through his forehead that whatever he had to say couldn't be good.

And Lucy really, really preferred good.

Graham didn't usually have to count to ten when dealing with Mattie, but Lucy Grayson might be harder for him to handle than his five-year-old daughter.

He couldn't shake the sight of Hunter and Lucy standing so close when he'd walked into the front office. What had they been doing? There had to be a good explanation for why they'd been tangled up together. For why Hunter had been behind the receptionist desk in the first place.

Had to be.

"What were you just doing?" Though he attempted to keep calm, his voice dripped with irritation. And then, instead of giving her time to answer, the rest of his thoughts spilled out without permission. "I walked down the hall to find you practically in a patient's arms, and a young man at that. How do you think that looks? What kind of reputation do you think that gives the office?"

Her mouth opened but no words came out.

Didn't she have anything to say to defend herself? And why did *she* look upset with *him*?

A glance over his shoulder told him Hunter was in the exam room, door closed. Waiting. Graham couldn't deal with Lucy right now. His patient needed sutures and that came first.

He faced her again. "I need to help Hunter." Plus, he needed to finish this appointment in time to grab Mattie from school so she didn't have to ride the bus. He knew she didn't like it, though she rarely complained. His daughter seemed to think it was her job to take care of him instead of his job to protect her.

"But I—" Lucy had finally found her voice. "I wasn't—"

"We'll talk about this later."

Without letting her finish, Graham turned and walked down the hall. Exasperation snaked under his collar, mixed with a faint touch of guilt for being so short with Lucy. He paused outside the door to exam room two, loosening the knot of his tie. Somehow, he needed to get his mind out of the fog that had descended on him this morning.

For being a Tuesday, today definitely felt like a Monday.

Nothing was going according to plan. First, he'd wanted a qualified person to fill in for Hollie. Instead, he'd got Lucy. He'd known after their conversation Sunday night that Lucy didn't have any experience working in a medical office. Her résumé sounded like an audition for a Broadway show. Yet he'd been desperate. And he knew she was, too.

That, coupled with the pressure from Olivia, had prompted him to give working with Lucy a shot.

No pun intended.

The morning had been crazy busy, and Graham hadn't really had time to observe Lucy. Except for the time he'd found her dancing in her chair, their close encounter by the charts…and then finding her and Hunter behind the desk together.

The unprofessional nature of what he'd seen grated. Graham had the niggling sense that he was missing some piece of the puzzle with Lucy. When he'd questioned her about previous employment on Sunday night, Lucy had been vague. She'd mentioned working at a dance school back in Colorado. Until…what? She hadn't really said why she'd left. Only something about a "difference of opinion" with the owners of the studio. Now he wondered if there was more to the story. Had she been unprofessional there? What had gone on between them?

It was obviously something he needed to figure out. Along with whether he'd made a bad choice in hiring her. Did he need to let her go already?

The thought came with an underlying sense of relief. Why?

Graham didn't want to go anywhere near the answer to that question, because if he did, he'd have to analyze the fact that Lucy Grayson flustered him. She was…young. Flighty. And entirely too beautiful for her own good.

If Brooke were still alive, she'd never be okay with someone like Lucy working in his front office. Graham wouldn't be, either. But Brooke was gone. And Graham should be able to have a receptionist without thinking of her as anything but that.

Only, seeing Lucy in Hunter's arms…something had sparked in Graham that he hadn't expected. A sense of jealousy. Where had it come from? He didn't know. Nor did he want to explore it.

Lucy might be a good fill-in for Hollie on maternity leave, or she might not. The jury on that was still out. But as for any attraction Graham felt for the young woman?

That, he knew his answer to. He'd already had the love of his life. Dating, marriage, love…those things weren't for him. Which meant attraction to his off-limits receptionist wasn't an option.

Chapter Three

Lucy pushed out the doors of the medical office and screamed up at the mocking bright blue sky. *Oh, my.* Her heartbeats settled from outraged racing to annoyed drumming. That scream had felt good. She'd like to indulge in one more—this time in Graham's presence. But he was still dealing with Hunter.

After Graham had headed down the hall, Lucy stayed until it was time to turn the phones over to the answering service. Then she'd waved goodbye to Danielle—who probably thought she was just ducking out to grab something for lunch—and headed outside.

She didn't want to leave the only real job option she had in this town, but Lucy knew better than to let someone treat her the way Graham just had. His accusations had stolen the air from her lungs and the words from her mouth.

She and Hunter had been totally innocent in that situation, yet Graham assumed the worst.

Lucy didn't like thinking a person was one thing and then finding out they were something completely different. At least with Graham she'd found out right away.

Unlike before.

Words spoken about her years earlier tumbled back. She

could still hear Nate talking to his best friend, still picture his arrogant behavior.

After that, she's all yours.

Indignation flared at the memory. Lucy had vowed never to let someone treat her with such disrespect again. Her independent, take-care-of-herself streak had started growing the day she'd overheard Nate, and it hadn't slowed since.

Which meant she couldn't stay working for Graham. Not if that was what he thought of her. Not if that was how he planned to treat her.

She *should* feel relieved leaving. Instead, pinpricks of disappointment riddled her skin.

She needed this job. Too bad Graham had reacted the way he had. Lucy could see now he'd never really given her a chance. He'd thrown her into the position with hardly any training and then he'd jumped to conclusions.

It wasn't as though working as a receptionist in a medical office would end up on her Pinterest board for dream work. If Lucy let herself travel down that road, she'd wish her way into owning a dance school she could run under her own philosophy. But that option wasn't on the horizon.

Lucy paused near her car as a school bus pulled up to the parking lot. The door opened and Mattie got off, clutching some things to her chest.

Hadn't Graham said he was going to pick her up?

The bus pulled away, and Mattie dropped the items she'd been holding on to the grass between the sidewalk and the parking lot.

Lucy approached. "Hi, Mattie Grace."

The little girl glanced up, shoving her glasses to the bridge of her nose. "Hi, Lucy." One shoe was untied, but the rest of her looked perfectly put together. A bright, white shirt without a mark on it—something Lucy could rarely boast of accomplishing—a jean skirt, light-up tennis shoes and a pink fleece sweatshirt. The sight made Lucy realize she'd forgotten her jacket inside.

Double drat. Maybe she could live without it. After all, the weather in Texas was warmer than Colorado.

"What's going on with your lunch?" Mattie's pink-and-purple lunch box was open, leftover contents and containers spread on the ground. Lucy knelt, helping her put the items back inside.

"One of the boys kicked my lunch box on the bus and everything fell out."

At Mattie's quiet explanation, Lucy's outrage spiked a few degrees. "Sounds like I should pay a visit to your school bus tomorrow."

The girl's smile was like the sun coming out from behind clouds. "It's okay. He doesn't bug me very often. My dad said he was going to pick me up so I didn't have to ride the bus today, but he must have forgot."

Oh, be still her heart. No matter how much Lucy didn't like Graham right now, she knew he'd never forget Mattie. "I don't think he forgot, sweetie. I think he just had a busy morning."

Lucy barely resisted scooping the girl up in a big hug. They closed the lunch box and stood, slipping it into Mattie's backpack.

After Graham and Mattie had left the other night, Olivia had told Lucy that Graham's wife had passed away from cystic fibrosis at a young age—only in her twenties. Since then, it sounded like Graham pretty much worked and took care of Mattie.

As if her thoughts had summoned him, Graham came out of the office and jogged to his car, the *beep-beep* from his key fob interrupting the quiet. Since he was parked on the other side of the building, he didn't notice them.

Lucy and Mattie shared a grin. "Told you he didn't forget. Think we should stop him or let him go?"

"Let him go."

Lucy laughed. "I'm not sure whether to be impressed or shocked."

That earned her a giggle.

The thought was tempting. A trip to school and subsequent freak-out would serve Graham right. Smothering her impulse to let him suffer a bit, Lucy called out to him across the lot. He looked in their direction, shoulders sagging when he saw Mattie.

Since his adorable daughter was standing next to her, Lucy would figure out how to talk to Graham in a civilized manner. She would put on her maturity cape—at least, until no little ears were listening—and if she could manage it, beyond that.

He came over, dropped in front of his daughter and pulled her into a hug. Lucy ignored the tug on her heart. *I will not like Graham. I will not soften toward him.* When Graham buried his face in Mattie's hair and inhaled as if he wouldn't live another second without smelling her, Lucy lost the battle. The chant wasn't working.

"Did you take the bus?"

Mattie nodded.

"Why didn't you wait? I told you I'd come get you."

"It's okay, Dad. I didn't mind."

Graham ran a hand through his hair, causing the dark locks to stick out in every direction and reminding Lucy of a young boy. She skipped over the thought, concentrating instead on the irritation she'd felt inside the office minutes ago.

"Next time, just wait for me, okay?"

The small shrug told Lucy Mattie's answer was far more of a "we'll see" than a "yes." Lucy liked the girl more and more by the moment. If only Mattie didn't have that look marring her features. Lucy couldn't figure out if she was sad or serious or both.

"Why don't you go inside and find Danielle?" Graham spoke to Mattie. "I'll be in in a sec."

"Okay. 'Bye, Ms. Lucy."

So they'd gone formal. Lucy offered Mattie a fist bump, which she answered with a small nudge.

Graham watched Mattie go inside before facing Lucy. She fought the temptation to squirm, knowing she hadn't done anything wrong. It might have looked strange to find Hunter behind her desk, but Graham could have given her the benefit of the doubt. He could have let her explain.

Instead, he thought she was so unprofessional that she'd throw herself at one of his patients.

Lucy sent up an SOS prayer that she'd be able to talk to Graham in a mature manner and that God would show her how to handle this conversation. After Graham had walked away from her inside, Lucy hadn't even considered asking God for guidance. She'd just followed her instincts. She was horrible at remembering to pray for help, usually barreling forward without stopping to think. Certainly without stopping to pray.

But in this situation, Lucy needed all of the direction she could get. Because not only was she at a loss for what to do if this job didn't work out, she'd never been very good at keeping her thoughts to herself.

When Graham had realized Lucy was no longer inside the office, he'd wondered if she'd just left to grab some lunch…or if she'd taken off, never planning to return. After the way he'd acted, Graham wouldn't blame her if she had bolted.

Hunter had told Graham what had happened and why he'd been behind Lucy's desk. A very simple explanation. If only the sight hadn't sent Graham into thinking the worst.

He'd jumped to conclusions and been a jerk. Now he was going to have to grovel. The thought almost tugged a smile from his lips. He hadn't groveled in ages—not since Brooke. Though, even then, it had been more in teasing. They'd had a good relationship, not the constant back-and-forth bickering that some couples were prone to. Which was exactly why Graham didn't expect to have anything like it again.

But he did have a bit of experience in apologizing. What husband didn't?

"About earlier."

She crossed her arms, gaze defiant.

"I'm sorry for my reaction. I was short with you and I jumped to conclusions."

When she opened her mouth, he braced for her to be angry with him. Instead, like a slowly deflating balloon, her shoulders lowered. "Okay."

Not exactly accepting his apology, but he'd take it for now.

On to the second order of business. Before he asked her to stay, Graham needed to know what had transpired at her old job. But he had the feeling she wasn't going to like his prying. "Lucy, what happened at the dance school you worked at in Colorado?"

"I don't want to talk about it." She mumbled a word that sounded a lot like *mature*. After fidgeting with the collar of her green dress, she let loose a frustrated exhalation. "Why do you want to know?"

"If you're going to be working here, and I'm going to trust you, I need to know."

"But I'm not—" Her sigh scattered across the parking lot. "Fine. It's not like I did anything bad there. I worked at the same school for years and loved it, but when they sold to new owners, we couldn't get along."

"Why not?"

A man could spend years deciphering the emotions that flickered through her gorgeous blue eyes. Graham focused on her mouth instead, but that didn't help. Her lips pressed together, broadcasting frustration with his questions.

"They were so into the correct dance positions, they were cruel. I mean, I get that they wanted to win competitions. What school doesn't? But they pushed too far. They were way too strict on all of the age groups, but especially the beginner's classes. Those little girls are there to learn to love dance, not to do a perfect plié at age four."

"That's it?"

"Um, kind of."

"Lucy."

"I confronted them about it, asking them to change the way they were treating the students. It didn't go over well. They said I didn't have the right attitude to be one of their teachers. That's when I knew I couldn't continue working there, so I packed up and moved."

Huh. Graham had thought there might be a skeleton in her closet. Instead, she'd been a defender for the young girls in her classes. Wouldn't he want someone to do the same for Mattie if she were in a class like that? He'd definitely had Lucy pegged as something she wasn't.

This woman surprised him. And Graham wanted her to stay working for him. In one morning, she'd accomplished more than any of the temps. His patients even liked her, and they reacted to change as though he was trying to personally offend them.

"Lucy, will you consider coming back to work?"

She rubbed her arms. "I'm not a huge fan of yours right now."

"I'm not a huge fan of myself right now."

Those lips curved ever so slightly. "You know, I wasn't doing anything inappropriate with Hunter. I'd been standing on the chair—"

"I know. He told me. I overreacted." *And seeing his hands on you*…hadn't bothered Graham in the least. Lucy was too young for him to be thinking about her in that way. Plus, besides his other list of reasons, she was his employee. *Possibly* his employee.

"I'll get a stool."

Her head tilted, loose curls cascading over her right

shoulder as she studied him. "Why do you want me to stay, anyway?"

"You dealt with this morning's chaos better than the temps I've had in, and they had experience. All I've heard today is how delighted everyone is with you."

Lucy's eyes narrowed. "But I didn't get anything done this morning but handling the phone."

"But you did handle it."

She didn't look convinced, but at least she wasn't running for her car. "I'm not exactly qualified for this position." Her hand flew through her hair with agitation, sending the locks bouncing. One finger pointed at him. "You can't just throw me into a medical office and expect me to have a clue what I'm doing. You have to give me some time to adjust and figure things out."

"I—"

"And you have to at least try to like me. I'm not asking you to fall in love with me—" Good to know since *that* definitely wasn't on Graham's to-do list. "But you could at least make an attempt to get along. People don't usually have such a hard time with me."

That was exactly what he was afraid of. Lucy had this energy, this essence that just attracted people to her. Graham felt the tug, too, though he didn't plan to pursue anything more than a work relationship. A friendly work relationship. That he could handle.

"I accept your terms."

"Really? You're not just saying that?"

He raised his right hand. "I pledge to not be a jerk." He winced. "I'll do my best. And I really mean what I'm saying."

Lucy's eyes began to twinkle. "Do you think we can get one purse a month thrown into my salary?"

"No."

"How about one for the whole of Hollie's maternity leave?"

"No." His lips twitched.

"We could call it a briefcase, make it a business expense."

"Lucy." He groaned. What was he going to do with this woman? He wasn't sure whether to laugh or run in the other direction.

Her shoulders inched up. "I would try to keep bargaining for more, but we both know I'm not that valuable of a commodity. I don't want to ruin my chances."

He had a feeling she would be more valuable—to his office—than she realized. Now that he was over his misconceptions, Graham felt relieved he'd found a fill-in for Hollie that his patients liked.

"I think we should shake on it. Graham Redmond, you promise to be patient with me as I figure out this job—*and* give me a real chance this time—and I'll do my best to be professional."

Lucy offered her hand.

"I already pledged an oath."

She raised one eyebrow, waiting.

Fine. Graham would shake on it. He cupped her hand in his. It was warm and soft and definitely didn't make him think about a business deal.

He pulled his hand back. Scrubbed it against his pants.

She was right. He hadn't really given her a chance. He'd been expecting her to fail. But Graham should know by now he was the one who excelled in the failure department.

He'd definitely made mistakes with Brooke. He'd loved her. That much he'd got right. But he hadn't been able to save her. He'd known when he married Brooke there were risks. She'd had cystic fibrosis, but she'd been on medication and always done well. Until her lungs had got worse and worse. Even then, Graham had assumed he could help her, that she'd get better.

They'd married young—just out of college. She'd worked, putting him through medical school. And then they'd found out Brooke was unexpectedly pregnant. At first, Graham had been shocked. He'd been a wreck. Would Brooke's body handle the pregnancy okay? How would they make it? How would he provide? He'd planned to quit medical school until Brooke had given him a verbal slap, knocking him back to reality. She'd told him it would be fine.

And she'd been right.

At least for a while. They'd welcomed Mattie into the world, and Graham had fallen for her just as he had her mother. The years of residency had begun. Brooke had been a rock. Working, taking care of Mattie and shining like never before. Motherhood had fit her. Both of their parents had helped out as much as they could while living over an hour away. Things had settled in again. He'd been months from finishing his residency when Brooke got sick.

Graham should have been able to save her. He should have had the knowledge. He'd pushed her doctors for every detail, searched for answers himself—any treatment options they might be missing. But in the end, it hadn't been enough. He hadn't been enough. She'd faded quickly, no matter what he'd done. No matter what he'd prayed.

He still didn't know how he'd made it through those last months of residency without her. Prayers and family had carried him. Graham had come out stumbling. He'd followed through on his and Brooke's plan to move back to Fredericksburg and open a clinic near both of their parents, missing her as though part of his heart had been surgically removed.

He'd done it for Mattie. Graham would do anything for Mattie. Which was why he'd continued to practice medicine while doubts about his abilities as a doctor assailed him.

If he thought too much about Brooke, about how he'd failed her and been unable to save her, then he wanted to crawl into bed and never come out.

Instead, Graham focused on Mattie. Her needs before his. He kept putting one foot in front of the other, hoping the whole town wouldn't notice he'd fallen flat on his face two years before.

"You still with me, Hollywood?" Lucy's question interrupted his sprint down memory lane. She'd moved closer, about a foot away, bringing the scent of lime and coconut with her.

"Hollywood?"

Her lips lifted. "So, you *can* hear me. I wasn't sure for a minute."

A light breeze tousled her hair, and Lucy pulled her curls to one side while the hem of her skirt flitted above her knees.

For a second, Graham questioned his sanity, asking Lucy to keep working for him. He only knew his decision had nothing to do with her looks and everything to do with his medical office. Lucy was good at the position—okay, maybe *good* was too strong a word at this point. She had the potential to do well, and that was what mattered.

Besides, it wasn't as if he was in love with the woman. He could simply admit she was beautiful and leave it at that. Anyone meeting Lucy would think the same.

Relief slid down his spine. A bit of attraction? That he could handle. He wasn't signing up for anything more than a businesslike friendship with Lucy Grayson.

Graham and Lucy started walking toward the office, Lucy a few steps in front of him. Without permission, his eyes slid down her belted dress, noticing the way it hugged her curves and showcased her legs. He quickly bounced his gaze to the sky and bit back a groan. The outfit was professional, he would give her that. But it was also distracting. To him. He was positive Hunter hadn't minded rescuing Lucy, though the man hadn't seemed as frazzled by the incident as Graham had been.

"You know, you could wear scrubs if you want. A lot of people working in medical offices do. It simplifies things."

Plus, maybe scrubs would help keep his thoughts focused on work instead of on the woman in front of him.

"Scrubs?" Lucy turned back, nose wrinkled. "I'm not really a scrubs kind of girl. I think I'll pass."

That was exactly what he'd feared.

Chapter Four

Before Lucy could even consider teaching her first Saturday-morning beginner's ballet class, she needed two things—a Diet Coke and her sunglasses.

Assuming she'd left her sunglasses at work yesterday, since they weren't on the floor of her car, Lucy had left early enough to swing by Graham's office this morning and then hit the drive-through. Some things were worth the sacrifice of a few minutes of lost sleep.

Graham had given her a key to the office on Wednesday, which she considered his peace offering after their confrontation Tuesday. The rest of the week they'd been cordial to each other. Lucy had been scrambling to learn about the job, and Graham had been Mr. Polite. He'd been patient with her and completely professional. He treated her the way she saw him treat everyone else—very respectfully. It bored her just a titch, and Lucy had *almost* found herself wishing for the snarly Graham back, if only for the entertainment value.

She pulled into the lot of the small redbrick building, surprised to see Graham's car there. Did he work Saturdays, too?

Lucy parked and walked inside, calling out her arrival. When no one answered, she checked the reception desk.

Score. Her favorite Ray-Ban sunglasses—red on the front, multicolored on the inside—were peeking out from under some papers. She grabbed them.

"Hi, Lucy."

She placed a hand over her thudding heart and turned. "Hey, Mattie. What are you up to?"

"I was drawing in Daddy's office. He's working."

Huh. That did not sound like a fun Saturday to Lucy.

"What are you wearing?" Mattie's eyes traveled the length of Lucy's dance sweatshirt, striped fitted shirt that landed just past her hips, leggings and bright green Converse high-tops.

"Clothes for teaching dance. Except for the shoes. Those I have to change when I get there because you can't wear ballet shoes on the street."

"You teach dance?" Mattie's eyes grew large. She bounced on the toes of her pink tennis shoes. "And do you wear the pink slippers?"

"Yes and yes." Delight had erased the seriousness Lucy had come to expect on Mattie's face.

"And you do the twirls?"

A pirouette. "Yes." Lucy stooped to Mattie's height. "Do you…do you want to take ballet, Mattie?"

She nodded quickly, then looked down at the floor.

"Have you asked your dad?"

She shook her head.

Why hadn't she asked Graham? In the past few days, Lucy had learned the little girl was a miniature adult—possibly more mature than Lucy—and that she always seemed slightly sad.

That last one killed Lucy. She couldn't curb the deep desire to make it better, to give the girl some fun. A little joy.

When Lucy had been ten, her uncle had died unexpectedly. Her dad had been devastated over losing his brother, and Lucy had taken it upon herself to cheer him up.

She'd done everything she could to bring happiness back

into his life. She'd put on plays. Performed hilarious songs. Made him funny cards and left him notes. Sneaked silly faces at the dinner table. Eventually, it had worked. Dad had called her his sunshine, and cheering people up had become her thing. She already read people's emotions quickly, so delving into helping them came naturally.

And Lucy just couldn't resist bringing some cheer into sweet, serious Mattie's life.

"I think we should ask him."

Mattie bit her lip. "Okay."

Lucy glanced at her watch. She wouldn't have time for her Diet Coke run if she talked to Graham about Mattie doing dance. But when a little hand slipped into hers, Lucy knew it didn't matter.

Her decision had already been made.

Graham heard a noise down the hall and stood from behind his desk. Hopefully it wasn't a patient popping in. He wasn't exactly looking professional in jeans, an untucked blue cotton button-down and brown leather tennis shoes.

More likely the noise was just Mattie. She'd been drawing quietly in his office, but she must have wandered off. He'd promised her they'd do something fun this afternoon to make up for working on the weekend. Being Mattie, she'd agreed without an argument.

He really did not deserve her.

He poked his head out of his office door and found Mattie and Lucy coming down the hall hand in hand. His daughter had been pestering him with questions about Lucy all week. Turned out Graham didn't know that much about her, so he wasn't much of a help to Mattie.

He did know that the past three days with Lucy had gone much better than Tuesday morning. They'd settled into a working relationship in which Graham didn't have a ton of interaction with her outside of work questions—and he was thankful for that.

In the past few days, she'd managed to lose only one chart (Graham had later found it filed under the first name instead of the last), and she'd shredded a stack of notes he'd left that needed to be added to charts. He was working on rewriting those this morning. But, beyond that, she'd charmed his daughter, made friends with Danielle and managed to deal with his sometimes crazy patients and make it look easy.

Lucy and Mattie stopped in front of him, some kind of trouble hiding behind their shared glance.

In leggings and bright green tennis shoes with her hair piled on top of her head in a messy bun, Lucy looked the part of dance instructor. Maybe she'd forgotten which job she was going to this morning.

"Graham." She paused to wink at Mattie. "We have a question to ask you."

Unease trickled through him. "Okay."

"Mattie expressed an interest in going to dance class. The one I teach on Saturday mornings is beginner's ballet. It would be perfect for her."

Perfect? Lucy had no idea what she was talking about. The only activity perfect for Mattie was yoga. Although she could probably pull a muscle in that. Something with padding around her whole body and no physical contact would do. But since that sport didn't exist, he'd vote no.

His daughter had a major propensity for getting hurt. The last sport Mattie had played was soccer. She'd ended up with a concussion. Who got a concussion in peewee soccer? When she'd begged to take gymnastics, she'd sprained her wrist within the first week.

If there was a competition for reading fast, Mattie would rock it. Or a spelling bee. She could totally do that. He should check if her school had—

"What do you think? Can she come to class with me?"

"I think you're good, aren't you, Mattie?"

Mattie stared at him, seconds feeling like hours. "Okay,

Daddy." Her hand slipped from Lucy's and she walked down the hall, her little shoulders slouching.

Graham rubbed a fist over his aching heart. He wanted to make her happy, but more than anything, he wanted to keep her safe. Sometimes parents had to make the hard decisions, and this was one of them.

"Are you joking?" Lucy's hands landed on her hips, and she looked as though he'd just told her she couldn't buy another pair of shoes all year. Guess it had been naive of him to think she'd walk away and let him handle his daughter's care without injecting her opinion. "You can tell she wants to go. It's obvious. Why won't you let her?"

"You're overstepping your bounds, Lucy. You don't understand."

"What I understand is that little girl will do anything for you—including give up a dance class she really wants to go to. You should have seen her light up when we were talking about it. She *wants* to go."

"Mattie struggles with athletics. I don't want her getting injured or feeling left out if she's not as good as the other girls." Rarely did he get heated, but right now? Not feeling so calm. "Plus, who are you to have an opinion about Mattie or question my parenting? You're acting like a sixteen-year-old."

"I'm offended for sixteen-year-olds everywhere. And you're acting like an ancient grump."

"At thirty-one, I am ancient compared to you. And since I'm Mattie's *old*, *grumpy* father, I get to make the decisions."

"I'm twenty-four. You're not *that* much older than me."

"I am in wisdom." *What?* That sentence didn't even make sense. "Age doesn't matter. I'm her father. It's my choice." Graham did the math in his head. "Wait—didn't you just graduate from college last year?" A fifth-year senior. The way Lucy acted, he could see her not finishing in four.

"Yes. Before I started college, I traveled with a dance team."

"And then you went to college after that?"

She nodded.

He was being a jerk. Again. Why did he expect the worst from Lucy? Most people wouldn't take time off and still go back to school. She should be commended. But while she might surprise him in certain areas, she was definitely driving him nuts right now.

They stared each other down. Graham wasn't planning to budge. He'd made his decision.

Eventually Lucy's stance softened. "Listen, Hollywood, I understand you're worried about her, but the class is really safe. I'll be there the whole time to watch out for her and help her so she doesn't feel lost or uncomfortable."

Hollywood. Why did she keep calling him that?

Lucy glanced at her watch. "I know you're my boss and all, but since it's the weekend, I don't think that counts. Do you?"

Strange logic. "Ah, I guess not?"

"Great. Then you won't fire me when I take her to dance anyway." Lucy headed down the hall, and it took a second for her words to register. When they did, Graham went after her. She and Mattie were standing by the reception desk, and Lucy was helping Mattie into her coat.

"You can't just take her. That's kidnapping."

Lucy faced his daughter. "Mattie, do you want to go to dance with me?"

Mattie looked at him with mournful eyes, then at Lucy before her gaze dipped to the floor. Finally, she gave the most imperceptible nod.

He felt like the worst dad ever. Especially since she rarely went against what he said. Must have been hard for her to admit. But even with seeing her blatant desire to attend ballet, letting her go was so hard. She'd had a lot of hurt in her life. Was he so wrong not to want her to go through more?

They were leaving. Mattie and Lucy were walking out the front doors while he stood there thinking. Graham followed them into the parking lot.

"It's illegal for her to ride without a booster seat."

Lucy marched over to his car. She wouldn't get anywhere with it. He always locked the doors. She pulled on the back door handle, and it popped right open.

Impossible. He *always* locked his car. That verse about everything being possible with God seemed to also apply to Lucy. Whatever she touched turned to gold. Did God just shine down on her life with rainbows and unicorns?

She grabbed Mattie's car seat and walked back over to her Volkswagen. After putting it in her backseat, she helped Mattie buckle in.

When she climbed into the driver's seat, Graham approached.

"I'm calling the cops. You can't just take my daughter."

Lucy shrugged. "Call the cops, then. The girl needs some fun in her life. You know I'm right or you would have already stopped me." At that, she slammed the door and drove off.

Turned out, Matilda Grace Redmond had some natural dance ability. And even if she didn't, the whole morning fiasco with Graham would have been worth it just to see the look of joy on the girl's face.

She'd missed a few steps—okay, a lot—but it was her first class. She'd improve. And, really, it wasn't about getting the steps perfect. It was about a little girl's delight when she learned the five positions and got distracted watching herself in the mirrors. The way she tried to stand on her toes the first time she wore ballet slippers, even though she shouldn't, just because she wanted to be like the older girls in pointe shoes. It was about falling in love with dance the way Lucy had so many years before.

When they'd arrived at the studio with barely any minutes to spare, Lucy had scrounged through the share bin—a place where dancers left items that no longer fit them—and found a skirt and shoes for Mattie. Total score. The dance school had a small area where they sold a few necessary items, and Lucy had snagged a leotard and tights there. A small price to pay for the way Mattie kept twirling in the outfit even though class had already finished.

Yes, the morning had been worth it. But now that Lucy was removed from the encounter with Graham, she really wished she would have handled things better. Niggling doubt about the way she'd acted snatched her joy at seeing Mattie so happy. Why couldn't she just be calm and reasonable? She'd always been passionate. Sometimes her emotions ran a bit…dramatic. She rarely thought too long before making a decision, usually jumping right in. But this time, she might have been a little too *Lucy*.

At least her intentions had been good.

She'd just wanted to help Mattie, not ruin her own newly improved relationship with Graham. Or hurt Mattie's chance to do dance in the future. She hadn't even thought about that. What if Graham never let Mattie come back and it was all Lucy's fault? That would be awful. Mattie really did seem to love it.

She sent up another of her trademark help-fix-what-I've-already-done prayers, hoping God could help her and Mattie out. They could certainly use some divine intervention.

Lucy corralled Mattie and Belle—the other little girl from class who hadn't been picked up by her parents yet—into the waiting area so that the next class could start. Just as they walked into the space lined with chairs and couches, the door to the studio opened and a female police officer walked in.

Panic climbed Lucy's throat. Graham wouldn't really… He hadn't…

The cop scanned the room, and Lucy broke out in a

sweat worthy of a marathon runner. Had Graham seriously called the cops? She needed a place to hide. But would that be considered resisting arrest?

Mattie and Belle were chatting and comparing ballet shoes, completely oblivious to Lucy's turmoil.

She dived behind the closest chair, body barely fitting in the space. She was probably overreacting—as usual. Maybe the officer had already moved on. Lucy leaned ever so slightly from behind the chair and peeked out.

Drat! The woman's black boots were headed right for her! She ducked back behind the seat, hoping the officer hadn't seen her.

"Excuse me, but are you Lucy? Lucy Grayson?"

Oh, no. Oh, no. Oh, no.

Lucy winced, slowly standing from her position. She was going to use her one phone call to call Graham and yell at him. As if she had actually kidnapped Mattie. He could have stopped her if he wanted to. She wouldn't have left if the man had put up a fight. He'd been wavering the whole time. Lucy had simply taken advantage of his indecision.

And now she was going to suffer the consequences. Lucy squared her shoulders. Time to take it like a woman. "Yes. That's me. I can ex—"

"I'm Peggy." The officer extended her hand. "Belle's mom. It's nice to meet you."

Lucy's mouth flopped open. Belle's mom. Graham hadn't really called the police. Yet… Lucy had just been hiding behind a chair.

"You are the new instructor for beginning ballet, right?"

"Yes." Lucy shook the woman's hand. "I am. I was just—" She glanced at the chair that had recently been her safe haven. "We were just…playing hide-and-seek."

It was the truth. Only Lucy had been hiding from a police officer, not Belle and Mattie. She could have told Peggy more of the truth, but *I hide from law enforcement* hadn't seemed like the better option.

Thankfully Peggy was gracious and didn't ask Lucy about her strange behavior. She did ask about Belle's time in class, and by the time they left, Lucy hoped she'd redeemed herself and her escapades would be forgotten.

Hoped, but didn't necessarily believe.

After Belle left with her mom, Lucy stuffed Mattie's ballet shoes into her own dance bag and helped her put on her pink tennis shoes.

They walked outside, and again, Mattie's hand slipped into Lucy's. The child still sported that dreamy look. One Lucy understood well. Dance had always been that place for her. Olivia had played volleyball, creating a bond with Dad, and Lucy had danced her way through life.

Even if Graham didn't forgive her, the morning had been worth it.

They got into the car, and Lucy pulled out her phone and texted Graham.

Are you still mad? She had THE BEST time. She's got natural talent. No injuries.

His reply came back in record time.

Maybe a little.

The man must have been glued to the phone. Remnants of guilt slithered across her skin. She definitely could have handled this morning better.

Lucy would have to work on that whole think-before-you-do thing.

I'm sorry I stole your daughter.

I'm still considering pressing charges. ☺

He'd included a smiley face? He was putty in her hands.

If it makes you feel any better, when one of the dance parents arrived in a police uniform to pick up her daughter, I thought you HAD called the cops on me.

Ha! That does make me feel better. Did she really have fun? She fit in okay? She didn't get hurt?

Overprotective man. His barrage of questions made Lucy grin.

"When are we going?"

"One sec, Mattie." Lucy had forgotten about the little girl in the backseat.

She looked so happy. Like she was living a fairy tale.

That might be overdoing it a little, but Lucy needed to plead her case a bit. She continued texting.

It's dance. There's not that many ways to get injured.

Not completely truthful. But at Mattie's age, the steps and classes were simple. The older girls had more chances of injury.

Any chance I can keep her for another hour? I think the first dance class deserves an ice cream celebration.

Crickets. No answer. Lucy glanced in the rearview mirror. Mattie was staring out the window. Patient, serious little thing.

Fine.

Graham's begrudging response made Lucy laugh. He didn't exactly sound excited, but she'd take it and run.

"What's so funny?" Mattie piped up from the backseat.

"I was just texting your dad that I thought we should grab some ice cream before I drop you off. What do you think?"

Mattie's eyes grew to the size of quarters, and she nodded quickly.

Lucy's phone beeped again, and her mouth curved, picturing another text from Graham. Directions on what Mattie could and couldn't do, most likely.

When are you coming home? I miss you.

Disappointment sucked the air from her lungs. It was from Bodie. Not Graham.

Bodie Kelps. Lucy had gone on a total of three dates with him back in Colorado. After which, Bodie had started talking about the future and Lucy meeting his parents. He'd even brought up the relationship-defining talk, which was Lucy's cue to exit the scene.

The move to Texas couldn't have come at a better time in terms of Bodie. Lucy liked him. They'd been friends during college and after, and she didn't want to lose that friendship because things hadn't worked out between them. She'd told Bodie in clear terms that they were not in a relationship and that she didn't want to keep dating after she moved.

But the man didn't listen.

He must think she was using moving as an excuse and he could prove his affection by continuing to pursue her. She wasn't. Even if Lucy had stayed in Colorado, she wouldn't have continued dating Bodie.

He'd texted her every day since she'd moved and called twice. Once she'd answered and talked to him—after all, she didn't want to be rude—but she'd tried not to encourage him in a romantic way. Her hints definitely weren't working.

Maybe she could etch it into stone or something. Although that would be pricey to mail.

Lucy put the phone to the side, started the car and drove out of the parking lot. Bodie could wait for an answer on that text since she didn't know what to do about him. He obviously hadn't believed her when she'd told him she was moving and that they were over. Lucy just didn't do serious relationships.

She didn't have some heart-wrenching story like the one her sister had endured. Lucy had just learned her lessons young. One time she'd attempted that whole *falling for someone* thing. The results hadn't been good. One time had been enough for her to realize she much preferred to love and embrace everyone in life without ever getting too serious.

Lucy had been young—her junior year in high school— the first time she'd been tempted to let her feelings for a guy progress beyond friendship. A senior had asked her to prom, and she'd accepted. He was gorgeous, and she'd let her imagination get the best of her. She'd started daydreaming about him, thinking maybe he was really interested in her, acting like one of the silly girls she usually detested. Then, one day after school, she'd needed someone to give her a ride home. She'd headed to Nate's locker to see if he could, but realized as she approached that he was talking about her to his friend.

At first she'd been giddy, thinking he must really like her. But then she'd realized they were discussing a plan regarding her.

They were talking about how long Nate would date her before passing her on to his friend who wanted a turn with her. Discussing her as if she were a piece of playground equipment.

She's already fallen for me. I have no doubt that by prom, I'll get what I want. After that, she's all yours.

If Lucy hadn't overheard, she'd never have known that

all of Nate's flattery and attention had only been done with one goal in mind.

Thankfully it had been early enough in the relationship that Lucy had come out of the experience with her heart still intact. In fact, she considered that day, that conversation, one of her biggest blessings because of how it had changed her life.

From that point on—after telling Nate exactly what she'd thought of his plans—she'd made a few decisions.

First, she'd started rescuing herself. She hadn't called her parents or sister for a ride home from school. She hadn't found one of her girlfriends and bummed a ride. Lucy had walked. Granted, it had been only a few miles to get home, but that had been the beginning for her.

No more looking for a prince when she could rescue herself.

And second, she'd tossed out serious (not that she'd ever had an extra supply in that department) and stuck to fun. She hung with groups of friends and even went to prom that year with a bunch of people. Guys. Girls. Everyone knew her. Most loved her. She loved back. Simple. Easy. No mess to clean up when she went through life with the objective of having fun.

"Ms. Lucy?"

"Yeah?"

"This really is the best day ever."

The contented sigh that came from the backseat wrapped around Lucy. Good thing she didn't resist getting involved with people in general, just dating relationships. Because she feared she'd already lost her heart to the adorable five-year-old in the rearview mirror.

Chapter Five

He missed his daughter.

Graham was a big sap, and even one more hour without Mattie felt like a year. *Pathetic* would be a good word to describe him right now. Even though Mattie was likely having a ton more fun with Lucy at dance and now going to get ice cream, he wanted her here. He wanted to look across his desk and see her at the credenza in the corner where she kept her art supplies and liked to color. He was selfish, that was what he was.

And he was getting nothing done.

With time to himself, his workload should be dwindling. But since Lucy and Mattie had left, he'd only dealt with a few charts and organized his pens. Who didn't want to claim an accomplishment like that for their Saturday?

He wanted to ask Mattie about class. Sure, he'd got some answers from Lucy, but he wanted to hear from his daughter.

Graham checked his watch. Lucy had texted only a few minutes ago that they were going for ice cream. He could go meet them. But that would be overprotective of him. Which he wasn't. He was more…curious. Another good word.

He grabbed his keys.

If he happened to be at the same place as them, nobody could fault him for that. And Graham knew just where his daughter would want to go.

Lucy judged the ice cream places in town by the level of excitement coming from the backseat. Clear River, a red storefront that boasted bakery, ice cream and deli signs, garnered the most response, so Lucy found a parking spot, and she and Mattie walked the short distance. If the smell of sugar and cinnamon that greeted them when Lucy opened the door was any indication, Mattie had impeccable taste.

Red booths with white tables lined the space, and a curved glass display case held mouthwatering treats with the menu hanging behind. When it was their turn to order, Mattie still hadn't decided which flavor to choose, so Lucy ordered first.

"I'll have a double-scoop cone. Chocolate peanut butter cup, strawberry cheesecake and… Let's make that a triple. One scoop of caramel turtle fudge, too."

She felt a tug on her arm. "Can I have that many scoops?"

Lucy imagined her answer should be no, but she didn't know why. "Go for it."

Mattie told Lucy the flavors she wanted and Lucy conveyed the order to the person behind the counter. She paid and they scanned the place for a seat. Once they grabbed a booth and slid in, Lucy tasted her ice cream.

"Mattie, why didn't you tell me this ice cream was amazing?"

The girl's small shoulders lifted. "I kind of did." She gave a shy smile and took a lick of chocolate.

True. She had squealed.

Lucy had thought no one could top Josh & John's—her favorite Colorado Springs ice cream—but she might be wrong. She'd probably need to return to Clear River and taste all of their homemade ice cream before she could make a truly informed decision.

Mattie pointed toward the front windows. "Daddy!"

Lucy turned to see Graham stepping inside the restaurant. He spotted them and headed in their direction.

"How's my girl?" He slid into the booth next to Mattie, and she threw herself into his arms. For a second, Lucy had thought he'd said *girls*, as in plural. And for a moment, her heart had leaped.

Strange.

"You have some kind of tracking device on me?" Lucy patted down her arms.

"Ha. No. I knew where Mattie would want to go for ice cream and I just—" He shrugged, then kissed the top of Mattie's head, accepting a bite of her ice cream.

Oh. He hadn't been checking up on her. He'd missed his daughter. A forgivable trait.

"You just wanted some ice cream?"

"Something like that." Graham's answering grin absolutely *did not* make Lucy's knees the consistency of Jell-O. She must just be out of shape or something. It had been a few weeks since she'd taught dance. "But it's almost lunchtime. Shouldn't we be eating lunch?" He glanced at Mattie's cone, then back at Lucy. "Instead of a triple-scoop cone?" His voice had lowered to a growl. And that was why she should have said no. "She's five." He raised an eyebrow at Lucy.

"They didn't have a quintuple scoop."

He groaned. "You can't have ice cream for lunch."

"Um, whyever not?" Lucy finished the caramel turtle fudge and moved on to the strawberry cheesecake. Oh. My. If she could marry this ice cream, she would. "Haven't you ever had dessert for a meal?"

Graham's head tilted. "No. Can't say that I have."

"We're going to have to change that." Lucy winked at Mattie.

"I'm going to get us something to eat." Graham pushed out from the booth. "Mattie, you're going to get a stomachache if you only eat that."

Mattie just smiled and took another lick of her cone.

Graham ordered at the counter, returning a few minutes later. When their food arrived, Lucy accepted the sandwich he'd ordered for her, digging in. Her first bite was absolutely to die for. She swallowed, wiping her mouth with her napkin. "What in the world is this sandwich? It's amazing."

"Smoked beef brisket on a jalapeño bun. They make their own sauce for it."

"What if I was a vegetarian?" She took another bite.

"I've seen you eat at work."

"True. You're forgiven for making us eat lunch. This is really good."

"Thank you." Graham's dry response made her tamp down a smile. He handed Mattie an extra dish. "Here, honey. You can put the rest of your cone in this while you eat some lunch."

Mattie acquiesced, moving on to her sandwich while Lucy dug into her purse and found some cash. "Here." She held the money out. "Will this cover it?"

"Cover what?"

"Lunch." She waved the bills at him.

"I bought lunch, Lucy. I don't want your money."

"But you don't need to pay for mine." Again, she attempted to get him to take the money.

"Anyone ever tell you that being unable to accept help or gifts from others is not a good quality?"

Ouch. Lucy lowered her hand. If anyone had ever said that to her, she hadn't listened. "Fine." She shoved the bills back into her purse. "Be noble."

His lips twitched. "Besides, I see that Mattie's in dance clothes, which had to come from somewhere. I assume you paid for those. Now I owe you money."

"We found some pieces in the giveaway box."

"And the other ones Lucy bought for me."

"Ms. Lucy," he corrected his daughter, shooting Lucy an accusing look. "And that's interesting information, Mattie."

"Does she really have to call me Ms. Lucy? It's so old lady."

"Old lady would be Ms. Grayson."

"Oy. Fine. Mattie, you're welcome to call me Lucy when your father's not around."

Mattie giggled, and Graham shook his head while swallowing a bite of his sandwich. "You really don't have a mature button, do you?"

"I hope not."

"Look, Daddy." Mattie leaned across Graham and pointed. "It's Grandma and Grandpa!"

A couple approached the booth, both looking as though they should be going to a business meeting instead of out for lunch. Mattie's grandmother was dressed in black dress pants and a yellow shirt, her perfectly styled brown hair shining, and her grandfather wore charcoal-gray pants and a white polo.

Mattie scrambled over Graham's lap to get out of the booth. She wrapped her arms around her grandmother's legs. The woman's hair stayed in place as she hugged Mattie back. "Honey, it's so good to see you."

She looked at their booth, gaze resting on Lucy, then Graham. "This looks cozy."

Cozy. Interesting word choice. But it wasn't so much what she'd said as the way she'd said it. Lucy rubbed her bare arms. She hadn't realized the temperature in Texas could drop so fast.

"Hi, Grandpa." Mattie hugged him, also, and he visibly softened. "Do you know Ms. Lucy?" Mattie's bubbling excitement regarding Lucy didn't transfer to her grandparents. Two wary pairs of eyes swung in her direction. And stayed. They didn't miss a thing, traveling from her messy bun to her bright green high-tops. She must look about twelve. Maybe fifteen on a good day. Perhaps Mattie's grandparents would think she was the babysitter.

Graham made introductions, and Lucy received some

polite nods from the couple, Belinda and Phillip Welling. Could their last name sound more regal? It definitely fit them. The name also meant they were Graham's late wife's parents, not his parents. That realization and the fact that they were looking at her as if she'd stolen their granddaughter made Lucy want to slide off her seat and hide under the table. Maybe Graham had called them this morning instead of the police. At least that would explain their tense faces.

Enough of this. Lucy could handle almost anything, these two included. "I'm Mattie's dance teacher."

"Mattie takes dance?" The woman's eyes widened before landing on Graham with accusation.

"She just started this morning," Graham answered. "Lucy's working at the clinic, covering for Hollie while she's on maternity leave."

This seemed to placate them somewhat. Perhaps the temporary nature of the position pleased them. Lucy wouldn't call them rude. They weren't even antisocial. There was just something about the way they looked at her. They almost seemed…hurt.

Lucy could totally go for a hole in the ground right about now. But a better option would be to simply leave them to their family affair. It didn't matter that she hadn't finished her lunch. Her stomach had suddenly turned. Maybe from eating dessert first.

Or something like that.

"It was great meeting you." Lucy pasted on her brightest smile and stood. "I'm going to take off."

"Are you sure? You're welcome to stay." Though he said the right thing, Graham's uncomfortable body language didn't support his words. He looked as though he wanted to hide in the same hole as Lucy. Only that would make them far too close for his comfort, she was sure.

He certainly wasn't confronting his in-laws about the way they were acting toward her. Not that she expected him to. After all, she was just the help.

Lucy would love to stay and keep feeling like a piece of gum stuck under someone's shoe, but she really did have to go.

She offered Mattie a fist bump. "You did great this morning." Mattie beamed, then switched to a pout with impressive speed.

"You're leaving? But Daddy's here and we're not done with lunch. Don't you want to stay?"

Her innocent question caused the tension in their small circle to triple.

"Actually, I've got to run. Graham, I'll leave Mattie's car seat by your car." No one would steal it in this town, would they? And with that, she bolted for the door. Once outside, she struggled for calm, but even the quaint Main Street didn't lighten her mood.

Lucy really needed to shake off that encounter. She knew better than to let other people's opinions affect her.

Back in high school when she'd overheard that horrible conversation that had reduced her to a pawn in a game, she'd instantly felt like a body—a shell—and nothing more.

She hated that she'd given Nate the power to impact how she felt. That was why ever since then she'd stuck to being carefree, to loving everyone without loving someone in particular. Because when things got serious, when she let herself get too involved, it gave far too much control to someone else. The encounter with the Wellings just now had brought back all of that turmoil. They'd treated her like an item that had outlived its shelf life and no longer belonged anywhere.

Lucy hadn't felt that unwanted in a long, long time.

And she'd do just about anything to avoid that feeling.

Graham felt as though he'd walked into a freezer. The way his in-laws were looking at him made him feel about two feet tall. What was going on? He'd always had a good relationship with the Wellings, so this scenario didn't make sense. They had to be upset about something.

He handed Mattie his phone, and she began playing a game while he stood and faced the couple. "Belinda. Phillip. What's wrong?"

"Are you…?" Belinda studied her perfectly manicured nails, then looked up, tears pooling. "Are you dating that woman?"

"Lucy?" Graham glanced from one wounded face to another. That was what was bothering them? "No. I'm not. Why would you think that?"

Belinda looked out the front windows to where Lucy had recently disappeared. "When we saw the three of you together, it just looked…" She trailed off and shrugged.

Somehow catching up with Lucy and Mattie after dance class amounted to him being in a relationship. Perfect.

"You already heard Lucy works for me. She took Mattie to dance class this morning and then I met up with them afterward. It was nothing more than that."

"How well do you know her?" Phillip's brow furrowed. "If she's spending time with Mattie, I assume you've checked her out?"

"Did I run a police report? No." Graham stifled his irritation at their unwarranted intrusion. "She's fine. Her sister is married to Cash Maddox." Though the Wellings were sometimes overprotective—even more than Graham—this conversation didn't need to continue. His in-laws should trust him.

Belinda touched his arm. "Be careful, Graham."

Of what?

"You wouldn't want to confuse Mattie or fill her mind with ideas."

In the past five days, he'd been closer to losing his temper than he had in years. "Trust me, I'm not planning to date. Anyone."

His in-laws nodded, and while their tension lessened, Graham's grew. "Would you…?" He forced out the words.

"Would you like to join us for lunch?" It was the right thing to say, but it came out wooden.

"Thank you for the invitation," Phillip responded, "but we don't have time. We're grabbing something to go since we're meeting with the foundation lawyers today."

The foundation. A charity started in Brooke's honor that raised money for cystic fibrosis research. One that always reminded Graham that he'd failed his wife. He knew it was for the best of causes, yet he'd never been able to help his in-laws with it when they asked. He attended only one charity function per year, and even that was a push.

The Wellings didn't understand why he wouldn't be a part of something that honored Brooke, why he wouldn't accept a position on the board. It had been the one point of contention between them. Until today. Now he could add Lucy to the list. Though that thought was absolutely absurd.

They said goodbyes, and Graham fought the annoyance churning in his gut.

Why did he feel so frustrated? The Wellings had only questioned him about dating—something he didn't have any interest in. So why did their interference bother him so much?

Graham slid back into the booth and Mattie put the phone down on the table.

"What was that about, Daddy?"

"How much did you hear?"

"Just Grandpa and Grandma asking if you were dating Ms. Lucy." Mattie munched on a chip, studying him with those inquisitive little eyes. "Are you ever going to marry someone, Dad?"

Graham had just taken a bite, and it lodged in his throat. He coughed, then took a drink of water. "I loved your mom so much, I really can't imagine that, honey. She was my best friend."

"Like me and Carissa?"

The image of Mattie and her best friend, Carissa, playing together made him smile. "Something like that."

"Only you kissed Mommy."

Good thing he hadn't taken another bite. He reached for his water again. "Right. When you're married, you get to kiss your spouse."

That seemed to satisfy her. Mattie went back to eating and playing her game, and Graham sorted through the day's events. Compared to their normal, peaceful existence, today had been rather crazy. And it wasn't even noon.

It seemed Lucy had that effect on their life.

The way she'd looked at the office this morning when she'd been ornery with him came flooding back. She did this thing when she was upset, though he doubted she realized it. She pressed her lips together, almost as if she was stemming whatever she really wanted to say from coming out. From what he'd learned about her, his assumption probably wasn't far off.

"Are you thinking about Mommy?"

Graham stole a chip off of Mattie's plate. "Why?"

"'Cause you're smiling."

"I was?"

Mattie nodded. Graham swallowed. "If I was smiling, then I was definitely thinking about Mommy."

At least, he should have been.

Chapter Six

It had been a week since the encounter between Graham, his in-laws and Lucy, and that freezer he'd walked into still hadn't fully thawed. It had warmed to refrigerator temps, but that was about it.

At work this week, he and Lucy had functioned *around* each other. Please and thank-yous had abounded. Graham had never thought politeness could kill him, but he was close to changing his opinion.

He'd dropped Mattie off at dance this morning—to Lucy and Mattie's delight—and Lucy was planning to drive her home after. He'd tried to refuse Lucy's offer, not wanting to add any more taking care of his daughter into her free weekend time. But the look she shot him had wilted his resistance.

Graham had let her win that battle. But when she got here, he planned to fix this thing between them. They had to keep working together, and he didn't want Lucy stuck in this place she'd been in all week. He kind of…missed the Lucy he'd first met. The one who did whatever she wanted—like taking Mattie to dance—and bulldozed her way through life.

Though that Lucy drove him a little crazy, seeing how she'd been acting this week threw him. He—or his in-laws—had obviously offended her. She hadn't said anything out loud, but her actions made it abundantly clear. Graham had noticed a lot less dancing in the front office than when Lucy had first started. She'd also been walking around sporting a *see how happy I am* smile that definitely seemed forced.

Even if Lucy didn't want to admit she was human and had feelings, Graham knew the encounter last week had wounded her.

It had messed with him, too. He hadn't realized his in-laws would be so upset by the idea of him dating. His own parents, who lived across town and whom he saw all of the time, had never given him that impression. In fact, his mother had started casually bringing up women who were single about a year after Brooke's death. Graham had ignored her at first. Then, when she'd continued to hint, he'd told her he didn't plan to remarry.

After that, his mom had stopped saying anything out loud. But he assumed she hadn't completely given up on the idea of making him "happy" again and procuring a few more grandkids. She had enough, between Mattie and Graham's nieces and nephews, but the woman was greedy.

Graham couldn't imagine wanting to date, but if he did change his mind, he now knew he'd have opposition from his in-laws. Brooke had been one of a kind—and their only daughter. He could have guessed his moving on would be hard on them, but he hadn't envisioned they'd react the way they had.

Good thing he hadn't really been on a date with Lucy. He didn't want to hurt his in-laws. They'd suffered enough already.

He heard a car pull up, and suddenly the dishwasher he'd been unloading felt like the most important thing in the world. Graham would rather unload a hundred dishwashers than face Lucy right now. All week, he hadn't brought up last Saturday's encounter with his in-laws because he'd hoped it would blow over. But it obviously wasn't going to. Which meant he needed to fix it.

He just didn't know exactly how to accomplish that.

Lucy pulled up to Graham's house and put the car in Park. The desire to let Mattie run inside without going in herself was strong.

Superman strong.

During the past week, Lucy and Graham had flitted between professional and uncomfortable. Meeting Graham's in-laws had put a damper on her mood. While she didn't know what exactly they'd said after she'd left the restaurant, Lucy could guess.

She wasn't good enough for Belinda and Phillip Welling. The thought that they might not want her around their granddaughter hurt. Lucy might be carefree, but she only wanted the best for Mattie. She wasn't trying to compare or compete with Mattie's mother. She just wanted to bring some joy into the girl's life.

Right now, Lucy didn't feel so joyful herself—a feeling she'd really like to shake. Hopefully the day she had planned hanging with her sister would chase away the strange sense of melancholy that had sprouted in her over the past week. She wasn't used to this feeling and she didn't know what to do with it.

She'd even gone so far as to pull out her devotional three times this week—practically a record for her. Olivia was great at doing her quiet time, but Lucy had never been able to stay on task when she attempted the same.

A knock sounded on the passenger window. Mattie stood outside the car, waving. When had she got out?

Lucy rolled the window down. "Yes? How can I help you?"

At her horrible British butler impression, Mattie giggled. "Why are you still sitting in the car?"

"I don't know."

"Okay, then, come on!" She ran toward the house.

As if life were so simple. Lucy turned off the car and forced herself to follow. Mattie had left the front door open, and Lucy walked inside.

Directly in front of her, a wooden staircase led to the second floor—where Lucy assumed Graham's and Mattie's rooms were.

Not that she'd be requesting a tour.

The living room was to her left. Wood floors, leather couches, a flat-screen TV on the wall and a small table in the corner covered with pink and purple Legos gave the space a homey feel. A large island was the only thing separating the kitchen from the living room. The older home had been remodeled…the charm of a midcentury house but with new amenities.

Graham came from the kitchen and met her in the living room, looking casual in jeans and a long-sleeved gray shirt. Lucy had got used to seeing him in business attire at work—dress pants and a shirt and tie. Unfortunately, she knew Graham's clothing habits way too well. By ten in the morning he loosened his tie, and by two in the afternoon he rolled his shirtsleeves up.

If Lucy was in an admitting sort of mood, she'd admit that she liked today's casual look on Graham. Truthfully, she liked all looks on him. Her employer happened to be a very good-looking man. Thus, the Hollywood nickname that had quickly come to fit him.

Only, today he looked a bit more rumpled than he normally did. His short, dark hair disheveled. Eyes sporting some red. Was he stressed? What about? Work or personal life?

"Thanks for dropping her off. I could have picked her up."

"It's not a problem. I was going by anyway, headed out to the ranch."

"You're going to the ranch?" Mattie chimed in.

"Yep."

"Can I come? I want to ride a horse."

Graham's hand rested on Mattie's shoulder. "Matilda Grace. You can't just invite yourself places. Lucy has her own life. She's got plans today."

Mattie looked crushed. Lucy knew her sister would be fine with Mattie tagging along. They didn't have any big plans—just hanging out.

"If your dad says it's okay, you can come."

"Please?" Mattie started tugging on Graham's arm. "I'll do anything. I'll clean my room."

"Your room's already clean."

"Please, please, please?"

Graham's exhalation ricocheted through the first floor of the house. Finally, after a few more jumps from Mattie, he nodded.

"I'll go change!" She ran up the stairs, leaving Lucy and Graham alone.

"I don't want her—"

"Getting hurt. I know. I'll ask Cash to give her a ride. You trust him, right?"

Graham nodded slowly.

"Okay, then. Why don't you tell Mattie I'm in the car? I can wait for her there and you can get back to…" Whatever it was he'd been doing. What exactly did Graham do in his spare time?

Again, not her business. She turned to go.

"Lucy, wait."

Drat. Escaping sounded so much better. With a supersized sigh, she faced him.

"I know things have been weird since last Saturday with my in-laws. I'm sorry they acted that way. I think they were just—" He shrugged. "They weren't very nice and I'm sorry. They're not usually that way."

Only for her. Comforting thought.

"They thought we were…" Graham looked at the television that wasn't on. He looked at the floor. Anywhere but at her. "They thought we were *together.*"

"Like dating?"

He finally met her gaze. Nodded.

So they hadn't been upset about her being around Mattie—though that sentiment probably wasn't far behind this one. They'd been upset about her being with Graham.

They must have thought she was encroaching on their daughter's turf. Lucy fought the desire to hunt them down and tell them she didn't have any plans to get involved with their son-in-law. The Wellings could keep Graham. Lucy would stay away from him as long as she got to continue having a relationship with Mattie.

"Well, I'm sure you set them straight."

He nodded again.

"There you have it. You don't need to apologize for them. I get it." Lucy wasn't Welling quality. She'd figured that out right away.

"It's not about you, Lucy."

Right.

"I told them I'm not planning to date anyone, because I'm not. I don't ever plan to remarry."

He didn't have to make up this whole story for her. So they weren't a match in the love department. The idea that Graham would never remarry was crazy.

"You don't have to explain anything to me. It's not like we *were* on a date."

"I know. But I'm telling you, I wouldn't be anyway. I'm really never getting remarried."

What? Graham definitely seemed the type to marry and grow old with someone. Lucy could picture him having more kids, a stepmom for Mattie. The girl would love it. Maybe having a mom again would take away some of Mattie's serious nature and let her be a kid.

What would keep Graham from considering marriage again? He was only thirty-one.

"Was—" Lucy tried to stem the words, but curiosity won. "Was your marriage…that bad?" Graham's frown told her what she already knew—she shouldn't have asked.

"No. It was that good."

Ouch. Why did those words sting? She hardly knew this man. She'd been in town two weeks, and yet his response made her feel as if she'd been shoved from a moving car.

This had nothing to do with her. Then why did it feel as though it did?

Mattie came bounding down the stairs and Lucy wanted to cheer.

"I'm ready. Is this okay?" Mattie pointed to her bright green, long-sleeved T-shirt that was covered in yellow and pink flowers. Coupled with older-looking jeans and scuffed tennis shoes, it was a perfect outfit for getting dirty on the ranch and riding horses.

"You look perfect, Mattie Grace."

She beamed and Lucy's heart did that gooey-melty thing she'd deemed "the Mattie effect."

It was good to see Mattie so happy. Lucy felt as though she'd been making progress with her. At dance this morning, Mattie had even volunteered to do the five basic ballet positions in front of the whole class, her face glowing with pride. While Lucy had befriended the girl in order to bring joy into her life, the opposite was also happening. Lucy was happier knowing Mattie. She already couldn't picture life without Mattie in it.

The thought made Lucy's stomach drop to the spotless mahogany wood floors. Graham's in-laws wouldn't try to stop her from having a relationship with Mattie, would they?

No. According to Graham, that wasn't what they'd been upset about. But Lucy imagined that could quickly change… especially if the Wellings saw her with Graham and Mattie again.

Lucy needed to be careful.

She'd have to keep her distance from Graham—as much as she could, considering she worked with him every weekday, Mattie now attended her dance class on Saturdays and they went to the same church on Sundays. Lucy didn't want to give the Wellings any more reasons to dislike her.

"We'd better go. I'll text you later about dropping Mattie off. Or you can always swing by and get her if you miss her." Lucy's mouth twitched.

Graham shook his head, though his lips did succumb to a slight curve. "I'm sure I'll be fine. I'll find…" He glanced around the living room. "Something to do."

"How about laundry?" Mattie offered. "We always have plenty of that."

"Thank you, Ms. Smarty-Pants."

Mattie grinned, gave Graham a hug and managed to fit in two pirouettes on her way out the front door.

Before Lucy could follow, Graham touched her arm, holding her there. She gently tugged away before he could feel the goose bumps that spread across her skin.

"I mean it, Lucy. I really am sorry for how they acted. You just moved here, but you already do so much for Mattie. She's so much happier with you in her life. I need to know you're not offended."

Graham couldn't have given her a higher compliment. The very thing she'd set out to do, she'd accomplished—or, at least, started to accomplish. Because Lucy definitely wasn't done yet.

"You do this thing when you're mad. Or thinking. You kind of—" Graham moved a hand to his face, then scrubbed it across his chin. "Never mind." He stepped closer. "Lucy." The way he said her name caused her stomach to do a backflip. "I need you to answer me."

Oh, he smelled *good*. "Why do you need this from me? Why do you care so much?"

"We were going to get along, remember? That was our original agreement." A slow grin claimed his mouth. "I was supposed to try to like you. And in that vein, I'd like you to be happy. Not offended by my in-laws."

Give me another whiff of your cologne and you can have anything you want. Lucy's eyelids drifted shut.

"Lucy?"

"Hmm."

"What are you doing?"

Her eyes popped open. Once again, *smelling you* didn't seem like a good answer. "Uh, forgiving you or your in-laws? I'm not sure which."

Graham brightened. "Good. I'll take it." He took a step back. Disappointing man. "I hope you mean it. Otherwise I'll have to make you take a vow."

Lucy knew what he meant. She *knew* he was talking about their previous oath, but the statement brought to mind wedding veils and white lace. He was never going to marry again.

Never.

That word held so much finality. It wasn't as though Lucy had thought they were going to date. And really, her views on serious dating weren't any different than Graham's.

So, technically, this conversation was a good thing. It just…didn't feel that way.

Lucy managed a strangled goodbye, then turned and walked out of the house. She made sure to walk slowly, as though to prove what she'd just learned in her conversation with Graham didn't matter. Because, of course, it didn't.

If anything, that feeling settling like cement in her lungs was relief.

Chapter Seven

Lucy and Olivia stood near the corral railing at the Circle M and watched Cash and Mattie take a few slow circles around on horseback. Mattie sat perched just in front of Cash in the saddle, helmet on, smile stretching from ear to ear.

"She's adorable." Olivia waved, and though Mattie looked as if she wanted to wave back, she didn't let go of the saddle horn.

"She is," Lucy agreed.

Cash rode over to them. "Mattie wants to go out on the ranch."

Lucy shoved her sunglasses on top of her head. "You sure, Mattie?"

The girl nodded, lips pressed into a straight line. Serious but determined.

"Be careful with her." When Cash leveled her a look, Lucy raised her hands. "Hey, I trust you. I just know Graham, and you're carrying precious cargo there. Plus, I don't want to get blamed for anything. I already saw a small scratch on her arm. I can't imagine how much trouble I'll be in for that."

Mattie had been practicing lassoing with a small rope and propped-up saddle earlier. She'd also thrown rocks, dug in the dirt and jumped into a pile of hay. Her nails had enough dirt under them to fill a sandbox. She was filthy and happy and Graham was going to kill Lucy.

Olivia pushed away from the fence. "Give us a minute and we'll ride with you."

"Absolutely not." Cash's comment cut through the peaceful day.

It sounded nothing like her brother-in-law. Lucy glanced between Cash and Olivia as they had an old-fashioned Western stare down. Cash sported a *don't mess with me* look that, although serious, made Lucy want to laugh. She had that tendency in uncomfortable situations.

"You guys want me to get the guns so you can have a duel?"

"Nope." Cash gentled his tone, but the steel underneath stayed intact. "Mattie and I will be back in a bit. Why don't you two head inside? Liv, you can rest." With a tug on the reins, Cash and Mattie rode out of the corral.

Rest? What was going on between the two of them? "What was that about?" Lucy studied her sister's profile. Olivia let out a strangled sound and strode toward the house. Lucy caught up to her. "Is there trouble in marriage-land?"

"No."

"That's good to hear. I've never seen him be so bossy with you. It was kind of marvelous."

Olivia's lips succumbed to a slight curve. "Not funny. He's just being his typical self."

"Meaning?"

They reached the front door, and Olivia stomped inside. She went into the kitchen, got out two glasses and filled them with water from the fridge. "Meaning he's being overprotective." She gave one to Lucy, then went to sit on the couch.

Lucy followed. "Since when won't he let you ride a horse? Isn't that a little outrageous?"

"Yep." Olivia rested a hand on her stomach in a maternal gesture. "It is, sort of. Except he has his reasons."

Lucy's eyes widened and she leaned forward. "You're not…are you…?"

Olivia nodded, glowing and fighting tears at the same time. "I'm pregnant."

Lucy let out a whoop and grabbed her sister in a fierce hug. When she pulled back, Olivia was full-on crying, rivers of moisture running down her cheeks.

"Uh-oh. Have you turned into a crazy emotional mess?"

Another nod.

"It's kind of great to see my big sister, who's usually so put together, falling apart."

"Brat."

Lucy laughed. "Tell me everything. Is it really not okay to ride a horse when you're pregnant? I didn't know that."

Love and annoyance warred on Liv's features. "It's not a rule or anything, but a lot of people say not to. Of course, I didn't meet Cash until after my miscarriage, but he knows how hard it was on me. He's turned overprotective—even more than usual. I feel like I'm under some kind of Cash-prescribed bed rest. Not that he's gone that far. He's just being careful, which I do appreciate even if he drives me nuts sometimes. And I guess—" Liv sighed. "He *might* be right, since I don't want to do anything to harm the baby." Smile lines framed her eyes. "But don't you dare tell him."

"I'm totally Team Olivia. We have the same blood running through our veins. That's, like, impossible to trump."

Liv's smile grew. "I'm only a few weeks. We just figured it out. I probably won't tell anyone but you and Janie for now. And Mom and Dad."

"Boy or girl?"

"We won't know that for a while."

"Please tell me you're going to find out."

"I want to. I think we will."

Lucy sat back against the couch cushions and propped

her feet up on the coffee table. "Now the whole—" she deepened her voice "—'go in and rest' comment makes more sense."

"That was a horrible impression of Cash. His voice is much more attractive than that."

"While I *might* agree that was a bad impression, I'm going to call a gag-me offense on the other part. Yuck! I don't need to hear any of those sentiments."

"You're really still a twelve-year-old girl at heart, aren't you?"

"Pretty much." Lucy would be offended if it weren't so true. "I cannot believe I'm going to be an aunt! We are going to get into all sorts of trouble together."

At Olivia's look, Lucy wiped the humor from her face. "And by that I mean I will be a perfect role model."

"You just might be. Watching you with Mattie is seeing you in a whole new light."

"It is? Why?"

"You're great with her. Almost…maternal."

What? At twenty-four, Lucy hadn't expected to hear that word used to describe her for a long, long time. She had no idea what to say in response to that. "Mattie's pretty great."

"True." Olivia's mouth lifted as though she knew Lucy was sidestepping the conversation. "I thought we could invite Graham over for dinner tonight since the Smiths are coming."

That would be the social thing to do. "We should?"

Lucy was excited to hang with Jack and Janie Smith— great friends of Cash and Olivia's. She couldn't wait to get her hands on their newborn daughter, Abigail, and see their adorable three-year-old son, Tucker. But did they have to invite Graham?

Her sister quirked an eyebrow. "Of course. What's with you, anyway? It's not like you not to include the whole county. You never leave anyone out."

True. And since she and Graham were *friends*, she

should want him there. Lucy was fine being friends with Graham. She just wasn't okay with losing a relationship with Mattie. And if Lucy and Graham got too close or spent too much time together and the Wellings found out, they would not be pleased. Lucy didn't want to do anything to upset them or have them disrupt her relationship with the girl.

"I'm beginning to think you have a crush on the man."

"What?" Lucy snapped her attention back to Olivia. "Why would you say that?"

"You're spending an awful lot of time with his daughter, and you're acting kind of funny about him."

She scoffed. "Spending time with Mattie has nothing to do with Graham. She's so serious, I just want to help her loosen up and have fun."

Olivia stayed silent.

"Fine. I can admit the man's attractive." Lucy ignored her sister's growing smile. "But attraction isn't the same thing as a crush. I'm not going to start sending him notes or anything—*Do you like me? Check yes or no.* I mean, he hasn't even pulled my pigtails."

Her comments were met with an exasperated sigh and shaking head.

"So, what happened between you and Bodie when you moved? Are you still talking to him?"

"Sometimes." Lucy shrugged. "There just wasn't anything special there."

"There never is."

"What does that mean?"

"You never go on more than two dates with anyone— three, tops. What's up with that? Why don't you ever date anyone?"

"I date all the—"

"More than a few dates," Olivia interrupted.

"I just don't do the serious thing."

"Why not?"

Lucy didn't want to discuss this. "I just…don't. Look what happened to you."

Olivia glanced at the wedding photo of her and Cash hanging on the wall. They were standing in the back of a pickup truck, kissing. Lucy didn't quite understand the reasoning on that one, but it did make for a great photo. Liv's hand slid across her stomach again. "I'm pretty happy."

"Yeah, now. But before…" Lucy didn't want to bring up all of this.

"It was worth it to get to him. All of that junk was worth it if Cash was the end result."

"Sap."

"Cynic."

"Me? A cynic? Impossible. I'm the most positive person you know. I might be the happiest person in the state of Texas."

"Then why the 'no serious' thing?"

"It's easier that way. I can love everybody, enjoy people, and I don't have to worry about…"

"Getting hurt."

"No! That's not it."

"Then explain it."

She couldn't. Lucy had never been able to. How could she explain what she didn't fully understand herself? It wasn't about getting hurt, like Liv said. It was about having fun and living life as an adventure. Taking each day as a gift and enjoying every minute.

"Have you prayed about it?"

"I pray all of the time." Especially when things got so out of hand she finally remembered God was supposed to be in charge of her life, not her. But Lucy was working on that. Hadn't she just made an attempt to do better this week?

"I meant about dating."

"No, not really." Lucy hadn't prayed about her dating life, but then again, nothing was wrong in that area. Why bother God with it?

"All I'm saying is that sometimes we head down our own path while forgetting to ask God what His plan is. It helps to ask first, then act. Maybe what God has for you is different than what you've decided. What if a relationship were possible with Graham? Would you be open to it?"

Heat burned in Lucy's chest. "That particular subject isn't one I need to ask God about." Unexpected frustration tightened her vocal cords. "Graham's never going to get married again. We just had that conversation a few hours ago. There's nothing between us now and there won't be in the future, so I don't have to waste any of God's time asking about something I already know the answer to."

"Okay." Olivia raised the palms of her hands. "I'll back off. I'm only trying to save you from some of the heartache Cash and I learned the hard way."

Why did Olivia want to push Lucy into the serious relationship *she'd* always wanted? Why couldn't her sister understand that they just didn't want the same things?

Lucy shoved up from the couch. She and Liv could have a conversation like this and still be fine afterward, but right now Lucy needed some space. "If you're pregnant, you must be starving. Do you need some grapes and cheese? To be fed like a queen? I'll get you something."

"I'm fine."

"Then you should rest like Cash said. I'm going to check on Mattie." Lucy tried not to stomp on her way to the front door. She pushed outside and headed for the barn.

That conversation with Olivia reeked like the stuff on Cash's boots at the end of the day. Her sister was being nosy, acting as though the decisions Lucy made were a bad thing. Olivia just didn't understand. She'd always wanted that whole true-love bit, but Lucy had just been less of a dreamer in that area. And she'd never missed it.

Only…hearing of Olivia's pregnancy had sprouted a small seed of doubt in Lucy. Didn't she want that one day? Babies? A husband?

Maybe.

She'd settle for a maybe. But definitely not anytime soon. Lucy knew in order to get to that point, she'd have to let someone in and go on more than three dates, like her sister had said, but she wasn't there yet. Just…not yet.

Lucy spotted Cash and Mattie riding toward the barn and waited for them to approach.

"She did great." Cash lifted Mattie down, and Lucy grabbed her, squeezing the girl in a hug. "I've got a few things to do and then I'll head in. Where's Liv?"

"Inside *resting*." Lucy put Mattie on the ground.

Cash shifted in the saddle, face wreathing in a grin. "She told you?"

She nodded. "Congratulations, McCowboy."

"Thanks. Did she actually listen to me about taking a nap?"

"I don't know. She got all nosy, so I came outside to find Mattie."

"Ah. Sister fun." He tugged on the brim of his hat. "Okay, well, I'll be back in a bit."

She turned her attention to Mattie as he rode away. "So, how was it?"

"Amazing." Mattie twirled in a circle. "It was like flying."

"I'm glad. Were you scared?"

"Nope."

"Brave girl."

"Daddy probably would have been worried about me, but he didn't need to be. I wasn't nervous."

Speaking of Graham, Lucy should probably check in with him and let him know things were going well. And she should invite him to dinner. She got out her phone and texted, then slipped it back into her pocket. She had to get over the weirdness she'd felt after talking to him earlier. So his in-laws didn't love her. So he wasn't getting married again.

So what? Unlike what her sister thought, she and Graham definitely weren't on a path toward a relationship. A friendship? Yes. But all that other stuff, Liv was going to have to let go of.

When his phone rang, Graham set the grocery bags on the kitchen floor and checked the screen. His mom.

He answered.

"You went out on a date and didn't tell me?"

"Mom, I didn't go on a date." He tucked the phone between his ear and shoulder and started putting vegetables in the fridge.

"That's not what the Wellings said when I ran into them yesterday."

"They saw me and Mattie with Lucy, and they assumed, Mom. That doesn't make it real. I told them I'm not dating anyone, especially Lucy."

"Who's Lucy?"

Graham moved on to the next bag, sliding whole-grain crackers and snacks for Mattie into the bin he kept for packing school lunches. "She's covering for Hollie, remember?"

"Oh, that's right. Maybe you should ask this Lucy on a date. How old is she? What does she look like?"

She's beautiful. And that has nothing to do with anything.

His mom continued without waiting for an answer. "I don't even know who she is, but I like her already. I have a feeling about this, Graham—"

He groaned, not that his mother noticed. Her *feelings* were notorious for being overly dramatic and wrong. Graham, his dad and his sisters teased her about them all the time.

"Mom, I'm unpacking groceries. I need to go."

"Fine. You can tell me about her when you come for lunch after church tomorrow."

Without agreeing, Graham said goodbye and hung up.

He grabbed the meat to put into the freezer. When his phone rang again, he answered without checking the caller ID. "Mom, I told you I'm not talking about this."

"I am not your mother. I am a snort."

It was Lucy. And she was referencing a Dr. Seuss book. His phone was a three-ring circus today. "What's wrong? Is Mattie okay?"

"Yes, not that you'd know a thing about it. I texted you almost fifteen minutes ago and didn't hear back. I thought maybe someone had abducted you. I figured you'd be on high phone alert in case I called about Mattie."

"I must have missed it while I was driving home. If Mattie's fine, what's up? Want me to swing out and get her?"

"Actually, the Smiths are coming for dinner. Do you want to come? You can just get Mattie then."

Surely his increased pulse rate had to do with seeing friends and nothing to do with the woman on the other end of the phone. Cash and Jack were some of his closest friends in town, though they rarely all got together. Graham could use a night of adult conversation.

"Sure. Sounds good."

She rattled off a time, and they said goodbye. Graham hung up and spoke to the empty kitchen. "There's nothing going on between me and Lucy, so everybody just leave me alone."

He left the rest of the groceries to unpack later and walked into the living room, dropping onto the couch. The photo album of Brooke that Mattie constantly looked through was on the coffee table. Graham grabbed it and opened to Mattie's favorite page. He ran a finger down the photos, sinking into the memories.

He missed her, but with each day Brooke was beginning to feel further and further away. Like a fading photo he couldn't protect. His mom wanted him to move on. The Wellings didn't want him to. Everyone had an opinion, making him feel like a piece of taffy stretched in every direction. But Graham could only deal with his own emotions. And he just wasn't willing to give Brooke up.

If he had his way, he never would.

Chapter Eight

"Your dad should be here any minute. In fact, we should probably wash your hands before he arrives." Lucy should at least make an attempt to remove some of the dirt from under Mattie's fingernails.

They went into the bathroom, and Lucy ran the water until it was lukewarm.

"I hope Daddy wasn't lonely without me today." Mattie lathered soap between her hands.

Did normal five-year-olds worry about their parents while they were out having fun? Lucy didn't think so. Just another reason this little girl was one of a kind.

"Did you think he would be? What does your dad do after work and on the weekends?"

Mattie continued to scrub the soap up to her elbows as though she were a surgeon. "Work."

"All of the time?"

"No. He also cleans, and packs my lunches, and goes to Grandpa and Grandma's house—my other grandparents, not the ones you met."

All exciting things. "What does your dad do for fun?"

Her little forehead crinkled and she finally slipped her hands under the water. "What do you mean?"

"Fun. Like does he golf? Run? Hunt?"

Each thing was met with a shake of Mattie's head.

"Watch movies?"

"You mean like *Frozen*?"

"Kind of." Though not really.

"He usually falls asleep during that movie."

"What about watching TV?"

Mattie perked up. "He reads."

Hmm. Lucy flipped the water off, and Mattie used the hand towel.

"And he watches baseball and football sometimes."

Sounded as if Graham rarely relaxed or did anything for himself.

Lucy's conscience raised its hands, screaming for attention. She wanted to ignore it the way she did laundry, but her passionate heart wouldn't let her.

Graham was exactly the type of person who needed someone like her to intervene in his life. Lucy knew without having to peek into Graham's windows that he was the best kind of father. She imagined he read to Mattie every night and packed healthy lunches and was übercalm all of the time. But did he ever have fun? Let loose? According to Mattie, not really. Of course, there was a chance the girl just didn't know, but Lucy doubted it.

Usually, she would be all about bringing a little happy into someone else's life. But diving into Graham's was a bit complicated.

His in-laws didn't like the idea of them spending time together, even if they weren't dating. So how would Lucy ever go about helping him kick back if she couldn't be seen around him?

Unless...the Wellings didn't know.

She could totally help Graham if his in-laws didn't find out.

Mattie flew out of the bathroom, and Lucy followed at a slower pace. She'd have to come up with a plan, though she wasn't sure where to begin.

She shrugged. She'd pray about it. She'd think about it. The idea would come to her.

It always did.

"Thanks for dinner." Graham set a pile of plates by the sink, and Olivia looked up from loading the dishwasher.

"No problem. I'm glad you could come. We'll have to do it again sometime."

"That would be great." Graham had enjoyed dinner. The smaller group setting fit him, and being with Jack and Cash was always easy. They'd reminisced and talked work, sports teams and family. Graham hadn't realized Olivia was pregnant. It had come up in conversation tonight, though Olivia had mentioned they weren't sharing the news publicly yet. Cash and Olivia both looked over the moon, and Graham was happy for them.

The memory of finding out Brooke was pregnant slipped into his mind. After he'd got over his initial shock, Graham had pored over parenting books. He'd thought he was ready for Mattie to be born. Until he'd held Matilda Grace Redmond in his arms for the first time.

Nothing prepared a father for that moment.

His heart hadn't been the same since.

Speaking of his heart, Graham should probably get Mattie and head home. The girl looked as if she'd been dipped in a puddle of mud sometime today and could very much use a bath tonight. But she also looked happy. Sometimes Mattie was so serious, so grown-up, that Graham forgot she was five and *should* be playing in mud puddles.

That was the kind of stuff he'd done as a kid. He'd ridden bikes with the neighbors and his sisters, and had stayed outside playing until dark. He'd come home dirty. And happy. Brooke had been raised differently, though. She'd been an only child, and the Wellings had been strict. When he'd first met her, Graham had thought Brooke would never go for him. She'd been raised with money, and he'd been raised somewhere in the middle class.

But Brooke hadn't been like her parents. She didn't have the same sense of importance they sometimes had. The kind the Wellings had communicated, probably without realizing it, when they'd met Lucy.

Graham wasn't a fan when they acted that way.

Lucy had said she forgave him and them, and Graham hoped it was true. He didn't want her offended. He owed Lucy for today. She definitely brought out a side of his daughter he loved to see. Sometimes he didn't know how to make that same little girl appear himself.

He should thank her, but she was with Olivia and Janie, cooing over the Smiths' newborn daughter. Graham didn't want to interrupt. Instead, he headed upstairs to find Mattie. She and Tucker had been tearing through the house all night.

He found the kids in a bedroom, a basket of toys spread across the floor.

"Mattie, time to clean up." His daughter looked at him and then went back to playing. Graham knelt beside her. "Did you hear me?"

She nodded. "I don't want to go yet."

"It's late, honey, and you've been here all day." It wasn't like Mattie to argue. She must be exhausted. Graham had heard about all of her activities earlier. She'd been flying high when he'd got here for dinner.

Graham started picking up the toys, and Tucker joined in without being asked. Mattie didn't.

"Mattie, you need to help."

She made a little effort, picking up a couple of things. After they'd tidied everything, Graham scooped her up. He offered Tucker a ride, which he refused, instead running ahead of them out the bedroom door.

Mattie's head rested against his shoulder on the way down the stairs. What would Graham do without his little girl? God had known what He was doing back when Brooke got pregnant. Having a piece of her left behind went a long way toward healing Graham on a daily basis.

He paused between the living room and kitchen. "We're going to take off. Thanks for everything."

Everyone called out goodbyes.

"I'll walk you out." Lucy came over, meeting them by the front door. She slid on a zip-up sweatshirt, then grabbed their coats, draping Mattie's over her shoulders. She opened the door for him and they stepped outside. The dark night sky twinkled with countless stars.

Cool air nipped at them, and Graham snuggled Mattie closer. "Can you thank Ms. Lucy for the fun day?"

Instead, his daughter lunged into Lucy's arms.

Traitor.

He grabbed his jacket from Lucy, slipping it on as they walked. At the car, Graham opened the back door and Lucy put Mattie in her booster seat, helping buckle her in.

She finished saying goodbye and shut the door.

"You're getting pretty good at that." He motioned to the car seat. "Guess stealing them from other people's cars is like a crash course."

Lucy propped her hands on the hips of her faded jeans. Tonight, her hair was in a loose braid over one shoulder. She had on her green Converse shoes and a T-shirt peeking out from under her sweatshirt that said Save Ferris.

Had she dressed casual so she could bum around the ranch with Mattie?

This woman was growing on him.

He pointed to her shirt. "Aren't you too young for that movie?"

Her eyes narrowed, lips curving slightly. Every time they did, Graham felt as though he'd won a prize.

"I like old movies."

"Ah." He rubbed a hand across his chest. "Did you just call *Ferris Bueller's Day Off* an old movie?"

"Well, it is."

"Now I feel ancient."

When Lucy laughed, that victorious feeling skyrocketed.

"So, did you have a good day? Get a lot accomplished?"

"I did." He'd expected to miss Mattie like crazy, but Graham was getting better about her traipsing off with Lucy.

"What did you do?"

"A little work at the office and some at home."

Lucy tilted her head. "Do you ever have fun, Hollywood?"

"What does that name mean?"

She grinned. "That's for me to know and you to endure not knowing."

Seriously. "Yes, I have fun." Not that he could think of any examples at the moment. "It's good to see you back to being yourself."

"How do you know what I'm normally like? We haven't known each other that long."

"It's not hard to tell with you." And it wasn't. Lucy was sunshine and rainbows on the gloomiest day.

"It's good to be back. I'm extremely delightful to be around."

He groaned.

"I can't believe you had most of the day to yourself and you didn't relax and do something enjoyable. What about a movie?"

"By myself?"

"Uh, yeah. Haven't you ever been to the movies by yourself? In the middle of an afternoon? You buy the biggest popcorn and the largest drink, a box of candy, and you settle in—" Lucy waved her hand. "Never mind. I can see I've already lost you. Looks like you definitely need some help in the fun department, Graham Redmond."

"That's not true. I'm perfectly content. I don't need any help having fun."

"I think I'm going to have to step up my position, from

best fill-in-on-maternity-leave office person *ever* to Director of Fun."

Panic thrummed in his veins. "Lucy—"

"Did you know there's a business in Colorado where that's an actual position? I would be so good at that job."

Was this what he got for wanting the carefree Lucy back? He'd hoped she would stop being upset about his in-laws, not make him her new pet project. What had he been thinking? Maybe he should go find the Wellings. They'd certainly put a damper on Lucy's good mood.

But even though the woman drove him a bit crazy when she was going full throttle, he did like seeing her happy.

He just didn't want her intruding in his life the way she was threatening to.

"Lucy." He took a step closer. Even with a foot of space between them, the close proximity sent his pulse flying. "I do not—" frustration over his unwanted attraction to Lucy caused his voice to drop "—want or need you messing with my life. Please. Tell me you're listening. Tell me you're not going to do something crazy. I do not need you as the director of fun in my life."

Lucy's lips curved, only this time, it didn't feel like a victory. "We'll have to see about that."

On Monday morning, Lucy laughed as Danielle Abbott, the nurse in Graham's office, squealed and waved her arms with excitement. In the way of nurses, Danielle was calm and put together under the most dire of circumstances. But today something had her in rare form.

"I have never seen you act so giddy. What is going on?"

"I thought we were going to wait a year to get married. A whole year." Danielle propped her hands on her ample hips. "And I was fine with that. At least, I was trying to be fine." She fanned herself with her hand, sending the tips of her short, red-orange hair flying. "Phew, I'm hot. Got myself all worked up."

"So, what changed?" Lucy heard the front door of the office open. She slid from her perch on the reception desk, where she'd been sitting while talking to Danielle.

"Come talk to me when you're done checking him in."

"That's cruel to make me wait."

Danielle chuckled, taking off for her back office area while Lucy greeted Mr. Birl, who was in for a gash instead of a rash this time. The man could come up with all sorts of interesting diseases and issues. Most of the time, he left without so much as a prescription. Lucy had once attempted to convince him on the phone that nothing was wrong with him. It hadn't gone over well. The more she'd tried to talk him out of it, the more he'd come up with. She'd ended up having to schedule him for an extra-long appointment.

After Mr. Birl signed in, Lucy grabbed his chart and walked back into Danielle's space. Large white cabinets and counters lined the sides for processing lab work, with a massive table in the middle that Danielle used for doing paperwork.

Lucy dropped the chart onto the table. "So, what's the rest of the story? What's up?"

Danielle finished applying lip gloss and tossed her purse into one of the lower cupboards. "We moved up the date of the wedding."

"Really? To when?"

"Two weeks from now. Twelve days, more precisely."

"What?" Lucy imagined she must resemble a fish right now, mouth flopping open and shut. "How?"

Instead of looking freaked, Danielle appeared calm and happy. "We've both been through really hard marriages in the past, so we were planning to take extra time with our engagement…after dating for two years already. But we finally decided we don't want to wait. I'm forty-four years old. I'm done waiting. I'm ready.

"We had so much of the wedding already planned that

we just needed a place. My uncle has a beautiful home near San Antonio, and we're going to have the wedding there."

"Oh, San Antonio! I've never been." There were all sorts of places in Texas Lucy wanted to visit. She could start there. Not that she was necessarily invited. She'd known Danielle for only a few weeks. "I'm not saying I'm invited," Lucy backpedaled. "I just meant—"

"Are you kidding?" Danielle came around the table. "Of course you're invited. You. Graham. Hollie if she wants to make the drive with a newborn. You're my people."

"Aww." Lucy hugged Danielle, and the woman's arms swallowed her up in a tight grip. Danielle gave the best hugs. "I'm so happy for you. Let me know if you need anything. I'd be happy to help."

"Exactly what kind of help are you offering?"

"Hmm. Well, I can't sew, so nothing like that. And I'm pretty horrible about arranging flowers, so that's out."

Danielle's laugh echoed in the room.

Lucy started checking things off on her fingers. "Can't sing, so no solos. Can't play any instruments. Oh!" She raised her hands. "But I can dance. If you need any lessons, let me know."

"You know, I just might take you up on that. Thanks for the offer, hon. I'd better get Mr. Birl into the exam room. If we get behind with him it will ruin the whole morning."

Danielle grabbed his chart and headed up front.

When she disappeared through the door, Lucy squealed and spun around. While drifting off to sleep last night, she'd been praying over how to implement her new Director of Fun position in Graham's life. This morning, the answer had fallen into her lap.

The two of them being invited to the same out-of-town wedding was a perfect solution to her dilemma. She could get Graham to relax and have fun, and the Wellings would have no idea she and Graham had done anything together.

Lucy couldn't wait to inform Graham they'd be going together.

She assumed he'd be *just* as excited as she was.

Graham winced at the knock on his office door. His head pounded as though someone had recently used it as a bass drum. The afternoon had already been long, and he was only two appointments past lunch. If Walt Birl tried to come back in this afternoon with another made-up issue, Graham wasn't sure he could handle it.

"Hey." Lucy poked her head inside. "Can I come in?"

"Sure." Graham unbuttoned his sleeves and rolled them up.

She checked her watch. "Right on time."

"What?"

"Nothing." Wearing black dress pants, a white shirt and red heels that matched her lipstick, her hair down and curling past her shoulders, she looked like all sorts of trouble. Graham definitely should have told her scrubs were mandatory.

To make things worse, she came over and perched on the edge of his desk.

After Saturday night at the ranch, Graham had come to the conclusion that he needed to be careful around Lucy. Keep a bit of distance between the two of them. Partly because he feared she would follow through on her idea to interfere in his life and partly because he just…needed the space.

He was having more and more trouble not being distracted by Lucy. Her involvement in Mattie's life and love for his daughter made it hard for him to keep his thoughts from running beyond friendship. But he didn't want his head going anywhere further than that in regard to Lucy, or anyone else, for that matter.

Graham felt a bit like a child stomping his foot, screaming that he didn't want things to change. But it was true.

He didn't. He liked his life. He liked taking care of his daughter and living with the memories of Brooke as his first and only love.

He would fight anything that tried to change those feelings.

Every day, when Lucy turned the phones off and left the office, Graham gave a giant sigh of relief. So the fact that she was inches away from him, looking beautiful and smelling like a sweet mixture of coconut and lime, wasn't helping his already testy mood.

Graham pushed his rolling chair farther from his desk. And Lucy. "What's up?"

"Did you hear Danielle moved the wedding up to two weeks from now?"

He dug his fingers into his temples. "She might have told me something about it this morning. I'm not sure I caught all of it, though. That seems really fast."

"It does, but she's happy."

"Good." He nodded. "That's good, then." If Danielle was happy, Graham didn't have to delve into figuring out why everything had changed.

And Lucy was in his office because…

"We're both invited, so I thought we should ride together since it's going to be down in San Antonio."

"Uh, no."

"Why not?"

"'Why?' is the real question. Don't you have to teach dance that weekend?"

"Dance is in the morning. You know that. We could leave right after class."

"Is this part of your get-me-to-have-fun plan?"

"No." Her arms crossed. "Okay, yes."

She really knew how to hold out. "Why would we need to leave that early on Saturday morning when San Antonio is only an hour away? What time is the wedding?"

"Late afternoon."

"So, my question bears repeating. Why would we leave that early?"

"We? That means you said yes, right?"

"No."

"I'll take that as a yes. We need to leave early so we can have an adventure."

The pounding in his head ramped up to jackhammer speed. "I don't want to have an adventure. I don't have time to have an adventure." Though he sounded like a pouty child, he didn't retract the statements.

"Too bad." Lucy pushed off the desk. "Do you need a prescription, Dr. Redmond? You look like you're in pain."

"I'm fine."

"And crabby." She broke into a smile and turned to leave his office.

His chance to get out of her crazy plan was slipping away. "Wait. I have Mattie. I can't even go to the wedding."

She paused with a hand on the doorknob. "I'm sure Mattie could go. But I also know your parents watch her. This town isn't big enough for secrets."

True.

"And are you really telling me that after Danielle's worked for you since you first opened the clinic, you're not going to attend her wedding?"

He huffed. It was all he had in his arsenal right now. "Fine, I'm going. But not with you."

"Oh, Hollywood. It's sweet when you get all cranky and think you're going to get your way." She beamed. "We'll leave after dance. I'll pick you up."

Chapter Nine

"I don't understand why you have to drive." Almost two weeks later, Lucy stood next to her yellow Beetle in Graham's driveway. As threatened, she'd appeared shortly after dance. Wearing a pink, short-sleeved shirt with skinny jeans, colorful heeled sandals and her hair down, she looked as if she could be featured in a magazine ad. She also looked far happier than he felt.

The weather had turned warm after a few days of not getting above sixty, and though the sun heated the back of his green polo shirt, Graham couldn't help a sigh. He'd dropped off Mattie at his mom and dad's right after dance, and the three of them were excited for a day together. He wished he could say the same about spending the day with Lucy. Four times he'd tried to break off the plans for going to the wedding with her. Four times she'd completely ignored him.

Stubborn woman.

He might not stand a chance in an argument with Lucy, but he *was* going to drive. He still had a swipe left on his man card.

"Listen, Duchess, you've already forced me into this day. I'm winning this battle."

"Duchess?"

"Yeah." Graham motioned to her. "You definitely have that regal thing going on where you expect everyone to be at your beck and call. You expect everything to go your way. You—"

"Enough."

His lips twitched. "Don't want me to keep going?"

"Fine." Lucy rolled her eyes and threw her hands into the air. "You can drive. I'll get the stuff."

What stuff?

She yanked open her car door, grabbed something from the backseat, then marched over to his car with her arms full.

Graham followed, wanting to repeat her eye roll about now. "What is all of that?"

She looked at him as though he were crazy. As though the overflowing basket in her arms was self-explanatory. "Road-trip supplies. What else?"

"Road trip? We're only driving an hour away, Lucy."

Her eyes widened. "Exactly."

"Are there games in there?"

When she avoided eye contact with him, he had the answer to that question.

"Maybe," she conceded. "But there's also food."

"I don't like it when people eat in my car."

She reeled back. "You have a child! Are you telling me Mattie never eats a snack in the car?"

"Every so often, but she's very neat. When we get home, I use the garage vacuum to clean the backseat."

"Are you saying that I'm messier than Mattie?"

How to answer that question without inflaming Lucy's already expressive behavior? When he didn't come up with a response, she let out a strangled "Argh." Her head swung back and forth. "Offensive on so many levels. You're just going to have to vacuum after me, too, Hollywood, because I'm bringing snacks. It's not a road trip without them."

"It's not a road trip." The under-his-breath comment set Lucy's lake-blue eyes flashing.

Graham finally opened the back door to his car, and she put the items on the seat. She faced him, confusion evident. "Do you have floor mats on top of floor mats?"

"Yes."

"What for?"

"The top one keeps the bottom one from getting dirty and ruined."

"That's the craziest thing I've ever heard. We can add 'neat freak' to your growing list of descriptions." She went back to her car and returned with a load of clothes and a bag. "My stuff for the wedding," she explained on her way past.

Graham had already laid his black suit, blue shirt, striped tie and dress shoes out in the trunk. One hand was all he'd needed to put his stuff into the car. Lucy, not so much.

"Oh!" She held up a finger. "One more thing."

Only one?

She leaned into her car and grabbed a bright orange purse. "Okay, now I'm ready."

Did she expect him to cheer?

Graham resisted another huff/sigh/whine/stomp of his foot. It was no use fighting Lucy. He just had to get through today. He'd endure Lucy's company and do his best to keep a nice wall between them. One with brick. And ivy. And a moat around it.

They took off, and a short way into the drive, Lucy started digging in her purse. She surfaced with an iPod.

He nodded to it. "What's that for?"

"It plays music. Graham, meet technology." Lucy held the iPod toward him. "Technology, this is Graham."

"I know what an iPod is, Duchess. I'm asking why your iPod is in my car. I have music."

"You know, I think you're meaning to annoy me with that nickname, but I kind of like it. I feel like it fits."

"I'm not surprised."

"And, in answer to your question, I made us a trip play-list. Do you have Bluetooth or do I need to hook up with a cord?"

"Bluetooth."

"Perfect."

"Did you say you made a trip playlist? Is that like making a mix tape?"

"Pretty much. Every good trip has its own song list. Then, when you want to remember the time, you can just listen to the playlist and voilà!"

"Why would we want to remember today?"

"Ouch." Lucy put a hand over her heart. "Are you always this crabby on Saturdays or is this especially for me? Do you need a cup of coffee or something?"

Actually, he could go for a cup. And he had been rather short-tempered this morning. He probably needed to tone it down a bit. "Why? Do you have some in that bag of yours?"

She grinned like a Cheshire cat. "I most certainly do." Lucy twisted between the seats and reached into the back, returning with a thermos and a paper cup. Somehow she managed to pour without spilling.

"Cream?"

"Sure." Graham watched her dig into the bag, this time coming out with a few small half-and-half containers. "Two, please."

She added them to the coffee, then put a cover on the cup and handed it to him.

"You're forgiven for bringing along all of that stuff in the backseat."

Lucy laughed and tossed the coffee thermos into the bag. "Where's yours?"

"I don't drink coffee."

His jaw dropped. "Is that an actual thing? I always thought people were lying when they said that."

She shook her head, but her lips curved. His pulse did

that annoying racing thing, which he ignored. "It's a real thing." She rummaged in her purse, coming up with a soda bottle. "I'm a Diet Coke girl."

"That stuff isn't good for you."

"And coffee is?"

"There have been numerous studies—"

Lucy plugged her ears like a two-year-old. "I don't want to hear it. We all have our vices."

True.

If Lucy didn't drink coffee, that meant she'd gone out to buy those supplies just for him.

"Thanks for this." He held up the cup, then took a sip.

"You're welcome." Lucy tipped her soda bottle to his coffee. "Cheers to our first road trip together." She held up a finger before he could speak. "And if you mumble something about it being our last, it really will be your last, Redmond."

"Yes, ma'am."

"I love this song." Lucy turned up the music and started singing along. "Waited till I had some fun. Don't know why you didn't run. Left you by the house of sun."

"Those aren't the words."

"Who cares?" Lucy continued to sing loudly. "But I wanted to break away. Wished that I could play again. Like I did in the band."

"Me. I care." Graham's comment was drowned out, and despite his total annoyance with the woman next to him, he started to laugh. She was so far off, the phrases didn't even make sense.

"Come on—sing along." Lucy held her soda bottle to his mouth like a microphone.

"No way."

"I'm telling you, you are going to remember this trip whenever you hear this music."

She went back to her off-key singing, and for once, Graham had to admit she was right.

Every time he heard this song, he would think about Lucy and how she looked at this moment, singing her loudest, completely content to ride in a car all day with her snacks and supplies.

She paused from her singing when the next song started. "What's my girl up to today?"

"Hanging with my parents. My nieces and nephews are going over later, too, so Mattie will not miss me one single bit."

"That's good."

"Yep."

"The question is, will you miss her?"

Graham stared straight ahead, hoping Lucy wouldn't notice his face heating at the truth. Because he didn't plan to admit to anyone that for the amount of time he and Lucy had been in the car, Graham hadn't thought about his daughter once. That had to be some kind of father crime or something.

His mind had been occupied with the woman next to him.

And he didn't know what to do about that.

"Admit it. You're having a good time." Lucy took a bite of gelato as she and Graham strolled along San Antonio's beautiful River Walk.

Graham had dressed in jeans, a green polo and brown leather sneakers for their day of adventure. Preppy. Casual. Distracting.

He scooped a spoonful of the hazelnut flavor he'd chosen. "I'm not admitting anything."

"Just look at how many things we've accomplished today, even having dessert before lunch. At least you can check that off your list."

"It wasn't on my list."

Graham definitely had that whole snarly/attractive act down. But the grin tugging on his features was enough of an answer for Lucy. He might not want to admit he was having fun, but she knew he was. They'd already hit the Tower of the Americas. The views had stretched forever, and Graham had been into it, admitting he'd never been before.

At the River Walk, he'd even forgotten to be annoyed for a bit, and the time had been relaxed. Their conversation flowed like the river, from Mattie to work to their childhoods, with easy silence in between.

Lucy was totally winning this day. She'd never seen Graham this chill before. He'd even teased her, smiled and laughed. Twice.

Which turned out to be problematic. Because the man could turn heads even when he was acting snarly, but when he smiled…*good night.*

As if to prove Lucy's point, a woman approaching from the opposite direction had her eyes glued to Graham. *Hello. I'm right here.* Perhaps Lucy should carry a big flag or something to remind people she existed. Not that she and Graham were together, but the woman didn't know that. She should assume they were. She shouldn't be checking out Lucy's not-boyfriend.

The woman tripped on the sidewalk—reason fifty as to why she should have been looking ahead instead of at Lucy's nondate. When she lunged forward, Graham somehow managed to cross the few feet to catch her.

She looked embarrassed, but also secretly pleased.

The tripping move had to have been planned. When the woman gripped Graham's arm for an extra second, Lucy resisted rolling her eyes.

This one's taken, lady.

She bit back the words. Not because they weren't true. Just because they didn't have anything to do with her. Graham was taken, all right, but by his wife. Just because Brooke wasn't alive didn't mean she wasn't in Graham's heart.

Lucy had heard the words come from his lips, and she

didn't plan to be so stupid as to ignore the off-limits warning. It was just the reminder she'd needed for keeping things light between them.

After Graham disentangled from the woman, they made their way to the car.

They got in, and Graham put on his aviator sunglasses. "Okay, what's next on your list?"

Lucy pulled the printed paper from her purse. "We don't have a ton of time left. We have to get to the wedding after this one."

"So what is it? I'll put it in the GPS."

"Well, I did a bit of looking…" She had a feeling this next part wouldn't go over well. "Have you ever been to the World's Largest Cowboy Boots?"

Graham looked at her, then out the front window of the parked car. "You're not serious."

"I am."

"You've got the Alamo as an option, and you choose the world's largest boots?"

"We don't have time for the Alamo. That'll have to be a different trip."

He groaned. Closed his eyes for a moment. "They're at a mall, right?"

Must have decided not to fight her. Smart man.

"Yep. North Star Mall." She rattled off the address and Graham punched it into his GPS. They took off, and Lucy hit Play on the iPod list that still had songs left. She wasn't a slacker when it came to the perfect playlist. She'd caught Graham enjoying the music once or twice when he thought she wasn't looking. But no singing—absolutely not.

Lucy could use some real food. She turned and dug into the basket she had in the backseat, pulling out some different snack options—chips (Graham frowned at those), some veggie sticks and two chicken salad sandwiches she'd put into a cooler lunch bag. Graham accepted his sandwich, and they both dug in.

After eating, he glanced at her with one eyebrow raised. "That was really good. Do you have a hidden talent I don't know about?"

"Nope." She finished her last bite. "I picked them up from The Peach Tree."

"But they weren't in the packaging."

"I was kind of hoping you wouldn't ask and I'd get credit for making them."

His laughter filled the car, creating a warm feeling in Lucy's chest. "Kind of makes you want to go on another road trip with me, doesn't it?"

He glanced in the rearview mirror as he changed lanes, lips quirking. "I wouldn't go that far."

"When are you going to admit you're having fun?"

"When you stop pestering me."

Lucy laughed and slipped her sandals off, putting her bare feet up on the dash.

"*What* are you doing?"

His tone startled her. "What do you mean?"

He motioned to her feet. "Why are you doing that?"

"It's comfortable."

"Well, stop it."

She shifted in her seat to face the crazy man next to her. "Why should I stop?"

"Because I just put on dash protectant, and you're messing it up."

He *had* to be joking. "Dash protectant is not a thing."

"Of course it is."

Wow. A giggle escaped. And she'd thought the floor mats were overdoing it. Still. "It's not like my feet are dirty."

"I wasn't saying your feet were dirty, just that they'll leave a footprint up there."

With a huff, Lucy dropped her feet back to the floor. "Anyone ever tell you you're a strange man, Graham Redmond?"

"No. Anyone ever tell you that you drive people crazy?"

"Actually, yes." Lucy grinned. "I've heard that one before." Her phone beeped, and she pulled it out of her purse. Olivia knew about the day, and she was likely going nuts without a steady stream of information and updates coming her way.

But it wasn't Liv. It was Bodie. Lucy hadn't heard from him in almost a week. She'd hoped he'd finally accepted that things wouldn't progress between them.

After typing a quick reply, she shoved the phone back in her purse.

"Here it is." Graham drove into the lot, slowing to a stop by the boots.

The size and quirkiness of them standing outside a mall made her chuckle. So worth annoying Graham for this. "They are ginormous."

"Yep."

"You could act a bit more excited about seeing them."

His sigh filled the car. "Fine. Wow. They are amazing. So large. I am impressed. Happy now? Can we go?"

"What?" What was wrong with this man? "We can't leave."

"Why not? You saw them. Isn't that what you wanted?"

"We have to get our picture by them."

Graham's head fell back against his headrest. "Lucy, we don't have time. We need to get to the wedding."

"Oh, come on, gramps. It will be quick."

Surprisingly, Graham gave in and found a parking spot without an argument. Lucy popped out of the car, waiting to make sure he followed.

They crossed over to the boots, and Lucy stared up in awe. She couldn't believe how huge they were in person.

"Picture." Graham growled the word near her ear. She was losing ground with him. She'd better make this quick.

An older couple stood nearby, and Lucy flagged them down. "Would you mind taking a picture of us?"

"Of course not, sweetie. It's always good to see young love. We were just like you once, weren't we, Arnold?"

Arnold didn't get a chance to do more than nod his head.

"We had the whole world ahead of us back then. Are the two of you on your honeymoon?"

Graham looked as if he'd rather be anywhere else, and this woman thought they were a couple? Laughter bubbled. "Something like that."

"Elaine, don't pester the children." Arnold's reprimand to his wife was adorable, as he was holding her hand and smiling while he said it. They had to be around eighty and so sweet with each other. Lucy didn't have the heart to tell Elaine anything but what she wanted to hear. Though where the woman had come up with the honeymoon assumption, Lucy didn't have a clue. It wasn't as if she or Graham had wedding rings on their left hands.

But if Elaine wanted to see a couple in love, Lucy planned to give her exactly that.

She grabbed Graham's hand and tugged him close, receiving widened, dangerous eyes as a response. This might be the most fun she'd had all day.

"We're not—"

"Oh, come on, honey." Lucy cut Graham off. "Let's get our picture taken." She handed Elaine her cell phone and went through a five-minute explanation of how to take a photo with it, then pulled Graham toward the boots.

The agitation rolling off him made Lucy's laughter build. He was going to kill her. Which somehow only made the situation more entertaining.

"What are you doing?" Spoken low and near her ear, Graham's words sent shivers down her neck.

"Play along," she whispered back. "I'm just having fun. Let the sweet couple see us happy newlyweds on our honeymoon."

"Lucy."

She tugged Graham next to her and snuggled into his

side. When his arm didn't go around her, she lifted it up and put it on her shoulders, then tucked back against his chest.

"You look adorable!" Their cupid was waving one hand as Lucy's phone wobbled precariously in her other hand. "Look here! I'll take a few."

"Smile," Lucy commanded. "Look at the camera."

She could feel Graham glaring at her. "No. You're lying to this woman."

Lucy met his heated gaze. "Graham, she doesn't know us. I'm just trying to make her day. I—"

"I love that with you looking at each other!" Their photographer was still snapping away, acting as if she were on a professional photo shoot. "Now kiss!"

"See?" Graham raised the arm that wasn't around Lucy. "See what you've done now?" He faced the woman, and Lucy just knew he was going to call out the truth and totally ruin the moment. It was just a kiss. Why did he have to make such a big deal out of everything?

Lucy put her hands behind Graham's neck and pulled his head down to meet hers. Just a quick lip-lock was all she needed—enough to satisfy Elaine.

But even with that logic backing her up, Lucy paused with Graham's mouth inches from hers. And then, before she could overanalyze, she went for it, pressing her lips to his.

Graham's mouth and whole body went rigid. Lucy braced for him to pull back and scold her, hoping Elaine wouldn't be able to see the truth of their relationship when he did. But instead of pushing her away, something in Graham's stance softened and his lips stayed on Lucy's.

It wasn't *exactly* a kiss back. But it definitely registered somewhere in the lips-meeting-and-staying department. Lucy didn't know what to call it. She only knew that while she was analyzing the moment, his lips were still on hers. They were soft, and the surprising taste and scent of Graham swirled around her, almost taking her out at the knees.

His hands traveled to her back, and Lucy let out a small sigh. Was he going to pull her closer?

All of a sudden she was cold. Alone. Her body swayed, and she opened her eyes to find Graham standing a foot away from her, looking as though he were standing in the middle of a freeway about to be run down by oncoming traffic.

He didn't speak. His mouth opened. Closed. Oh, man. She might have to take him to the ER. She could see them racing through the automatic doors, envision the conversation now.

He's in shock. Help him, please.

What happened?

We had an almost kiss.

Lucy clung to her amusement. She wanted to laugh. To think about the encounter as a typical Lucy decision and not dwell on the fact that Graham hadn't immediately pulled away.

She didn't want to think about how his lips had felt on hers.

Because then all she'd be able to think about was how she'd like to do it again.

Chapter Ten

What had just happened? Had Lucy just *kissed* him? "What was that?"

She winced. "A kiss. For Elaine."

"For Elaine?" His voice was somewhere between snarl and about to lose it.

Lucy took a small step back, palms raised in defense. "It was just—"

"That was quite the kiss, you two." Elaine shoved the phone in his face. When he didn't take it, she offered it to Lucy. "Here's your camera, sweetie."

Lucy was coherent enough to accept it. She exchanged a thank-you and a few more sentences with the couple before Elaine and Arnold left.

Why did Lucy look so calm? Why wasn't she as much of a mess as he was? And again, what had just happened? One moment, Graham had been arguing with Lucy, and the next, their lips had met. And stayed.

Why, why, why had they stayed? Why hadn't he stepped back? Grabbed Lucy's arms and removed her mouth from his?

Because he hadn't wanted to.

That couldn't be right. It had to be that he...hadn't kissed anyone in years. He'd been thinking of Brooke. He'd wished it was her.

Had to be.

When Lucy had yanked him down and kissed him, his first instinct had been logical. Back away and ask her what in the world she was doing. The move had seemed dramatic, even for her. But then, while he'd been contemplating all of that, he'd edged…closer. As if he couldn't stop his hands from sliding around her, as if she'd been made to fit into his arms.

His conscience and logic were having a huge after-party in his brain right now, raking him over for letting that liplock moment continue.

He knew better. Lucy might not, but he did.

"I'm sorry." His words came out strangled, as the situation wasn't really his fault, but he didn't know what else to say. Lucy might be Lucy, but he should have stopped her antics. And he was done wondering why he hadn't. Now he just needed to fix it. He needed it to go away.

"Me, too." She slid her phone into her back pocket. Took another step back. "It was just a joke that got—"

"Out of hand."

"Exactly. No big deal." Then why did she look sort of wounded and shocked at the same time? "We should go." She waved her hand in the direction of the parking lot. "Wedding."

"Right. Wedding."

They walked to the car in silence and got in. Lucy put on her playlist, and Graham punched in the address to Danielle's uncle's house on his GPS.

The whole drive, Graham kept repeating Lucy's words in his mind.

No big deal.

Not once did they feel true.

* * *

Lucy wouldn't mind a dance. They'd been at the wedding for hours already—from the outdoor ceremony through the dinner and now into the twilight reception.

So far her nondate had talked to everyone but her.

The whole plan to give Graham a day of fun had backfired. Since their kiss, he'd been unable to look her in the eyes. Not only had she *not* given him a relaxing day off, she'd moved their budding friendship back a few steps.

She stared past the makeshift dance floor under a tree strung with white lights and paper balls, toying with the napkin in front of her.

Danielle's uncle's place looked like something off of Pinterest. The massive lawn stretched from a tall, regal white house down to a man-made lake. A private lake hadn't ranked high on Lucy's need list until tonight. It was gorgeous with hints of sunset reflecting off the water.

"Ms. Lucy, will you dance with us?"

She turned to see two little girls from her dance class standing in front of her. The twins had been the flower girls in the wedding—Danielle's cousin's daughters, if Lucy recalled correctly. They were wearing white taffeta dresses and those little-girl high heels that nights like this were made of.

"Of course." Lucy wasn't going to let the kiss with Graham ruin her whole night.

They walked onto the dance floor and held hands, turning in time to the music. After a few minutes, Lucy's enjoyment grew. The girls were delightful, spinning in order to watch their dresses twirl around them. She joined in, making the skirt of her yellow lace dress do the same.

When the music changed and the tempo increased, the three of them broke out into crazy dance moves, and Lucy giggled along with the girls. She even threw in a few robot moves for good measure. By the end of the song she was feeling far more like herself. One mistake wouldn't get her down. She'd talk to Graham and apologize again. Somehow she'd convince him to forget all about her kissing him. Somehow she'd shake the moment from her mind, too.

When the song changed to Beyoncé's "Single Ladies," the little girls started singing along. Lucy bent to hear the words they were using, laughter bubbling when she deciphered them.

All the singing ladies.

Danielle came flying onto the dance floor to join them. "I can't believe this song doesn't apply to me anymore!" She glowed with a color makeup couldn't produce. Only a bride could pull off that look.

"I'm so happy for you." Lucy hugged Danielle, thankful she'd become a friend so easily in the past few weeks.

"Thanks, hon. Oh!" Her eyes widened. "We should have done the bouquet toss to this song. It's perfect. These are the kind of details that don't get planned when you do a wedding in two weeks."

"The wedding, the place, everything is perfect. I thought maybe you were skipping the bouquet toss." That part of a wedding usually didn't bother Lucy, but tonight, she wasn't feeling it.

Danielle laughed and shook her finger. "Nice try."

The music switched to something slow, and the current crowd filtered off, a new group taking their place.

Including Graham and the woman he'd been talking to for a while. Lucy watched them as she waved goodbye to the little girls and left the dance floor.

Beautiful, with dark brown hair, the woman was laughing at whatever Graham said. She wore a fitted plum dress that landed just above the knee, simple black heels and a pearl necklace. With Graham rocking a black suit, blue shirt and striped tie, the two of them looked as though they came from the same world and belonged together.

The kind of woman his in-laws would probably approve of.

Lucy glanced down at her fitted yellow lace dress that flared at the waist. She'd paired it with whimsical gold high-heeled sandals and a thin leaf forehead necklace. Earlier, she'd loved the outfit. Now she just felt out of place. Not at the wedding, but in Graham's life. What had she been thinking, trying to help Graham relax and have fun? Why had she thought she could be the one to bring happiness into his life?

Lucy walked over to the outdoor fireplace and snagged one of the blankets stacked on the short brick wall. The day had been gorgeous, temperatures hovering above seventy. Now the heat faded without the sun. With the gas fire pit and outdoor heaters going, none of the guests seemed to notice, though a few had slipped inside. Lucy considered it balmy compared to what she'd be enduring if she were back in Colorado.

She made her way down to the water, stopping to take off her shoes. Slipping her fingers into the heels, she continued walking, the grass tickling her feet.

A wooden dock stretched into the fading light. Lucy walked to the end and sat down, her toes barely nipping into the water. It was cold, and the temperature had her scooting back so that her feet no longer touched. She wrapped the blanket around her shoulders and tugged it close.

Her sigh echoed into the night, the pain that accompanied it surprising her. Unwanted tears surfaced as the events of the afternoon came rushing back. Mainly one event.

What had she done?

Lucy had always been adamant that it wasn't the fear of getting hurt that kept her from serious relationships. She'd fought with her sister over the very subject mere weeks ago.

But Olivia had been right. It was about protecting herself. It was about not letting herself get hurt.

Lucy could finally see it as the truth. But it was a truth that came too late.

Because her attraction to Graham was more than just

that. She…was interested in him. She liked him. He drove her crazy. He was insanely neat and detailed—the total opposite of her—and she wanted a repeat of that kiss.

More than one.

She'd gone from *I'm never getting serious* to *I'm in serious trouble* in one instant today.

"No." The word hissed into the night, joining the muted sounds of the party behind her and the silent lake before her. She couldn't turn a one-eighty like that. She couldn't go from nothing to having feelings for Graham, could she?

She went back through the moments in her mind, from when she'd first met Graham until now, including her sister's wedding last summer. Had it all started way back then? Seeing Graham on the dance floor with Mattie?

She had to be wrong.

Lucy wanted to go back to her innocence again, to believing she didn't date because of her desire for fun. She wanted it to have nothing to do with trying to protect herself.

But the kiss today—albeit an almost kiss—had shattered all of those beliefs.

Graham had a beautiful woman in his arms, but she didn't hold his attention. He'd asked Cherie—an old friend from school—to dance when she'd prompted him. It hadn't been his idea, and truthfully, he wanted to stay away from women in general at the moment. After what had happened with Lucy, who knew what would happen if he got near another one? But since Cherie had openly hinted…it would have been impolite not to ask.

So here he swayed, on a makeshift dance floor underneath a tree dripping with lights. Danielle and Scott danced together a few feet away, both looking so happy. Graham didn't know how they'd made the wedding come together on such short notice, but the place looked fantastic. Intimate and relaxed at the same time. The wedding fit Danielle.

She'd been with him from the beginning of opening the clinic, and Lucy was right. He'd never have missed this. Danielle meant too much to him. He'd danced with her earlier and told her that. She'd laughed away his sincerity, though her eyes had filled with tears. Graham had great people in his life. He'd seen God's presence and provision in so many little and big ways over the past few years. Losing Brooke had been horrible, but he wasn't alone.

While they danced, Cherie chatted and Graham halfway listened. Something about what old classmates were doing now. But the vision of Lucy dancing with the little girls minutes earlier stole into Graham's mind despite his attempts to shake it—much like that kiss.

Lucy was always beautiful. Graham wouldn't be a living, breathing male if he couldn't admit that. But in that moment, she'd been even more breathtaking than usual.

There was something about her Graham couldn't put into words.

She'd been laughing and acting goofy with the girls— not caring what anyone thought. Not realizing that every single man attending the wedding had his eyes on her.

When they'd arrived at Danielle's uncle's house and changed for the wedding, Lucy had got ready with some of Danielle's wedding party. Now she had on a yellow dress and a necklace that went across her forehead. He didn't know what to call it. It was delicate, with tiny gold leaves along the chain. With her hair down and loose curls flowing over her shoulders, she looked like a flower child. As though she should be running through a field barefoot.

But the dress didn't make her. She made the dress.

Graham didn't know what to do with her. He didn't have room in his life for Lucy. He wasn't willing to make space. Not that she was asking him to. He doubted she had any feelings of attraction to him at all. He was too old for her. Lucy would find someone young. She'd marry someday and have kids. But not soon. She had too much life to go out and live. Graham imagined she could easily bounce from city to city without a care. She'd be leaving the office after Hollie came back from maternity leave. And though she drove him crazy at times, he would miss her. He could admit that. But then he'd move on.

"Graham?" Cherie raised one dainty eyebrow. "Are you okay?"

"Fine." He shook his head, wishing the movement would clear thoughts of Lucy from his mind. "Tell me about your new place. Do you like it?"

"I do. I think I'll stay." Her hand slid along the collar of his black suit jacket. "Unless I find a reason not to."

The move made Graham uncomfortable. When his phone buzzed in his pocket, he jumped at the escape. He stopped dancing and checked the call. "It's my mom. I need to take this. She has Mattie."

Cherie nodded, and he escorted her off the dance floor.

Even if the call wasn't about Mattie, he'd take his mom as an interruption right now. As long as she didn't have any "feelings." He'd already had to do some quick explaining about why he absolutely wasn't dating Lucy but they just happened to be going to a wedding together sans Mattie.

Good thing his mother couldn't read minds. This afternoon's incident would send her into a matchmaking tailspin.

He answered just before it went to voice mail. "Mom? Everything okay?"

"It's Dad. Everything is fine. Mattie just wants to say good-night."

Graham heard the shuffling of the phone and then his daughter's voice.

"Night, Daddy. Are you having fun?"

His mouth curved. "You know what? I am. It was a good day." So he and Lucy had locked lips for a second. That didn't mean anything. And he had relaxed today, more than he had in months. Maybe years. "Did you have a good day?"

Her sweet sigh about melted him into a puddle. "The best. I just wanted to check on you before I went to bed."

Wasn't he supposed to be the parent?

They talked for another minute and then said goodbye. Graham ended the call with a grin. He loved that girl. Once again, he was reminded he already had everything he needed. He'd had the love of his life. And he had a daughter who slayed him with her thoughtful, serious little spirit and a God who watched out for him, orchestrating the smallest details.

What had happened with Lucy today didn't change a thing.

I don't like it when you're right.

Lucy pressed Send on the text to her sister and started to put the phone down on the dock before tapping her thumbs over the keys again.

It's really annoying.

If Olivia hadn't poked and prodded, Lucy would likely still have any feelings for Graham deeply buried and locked up. Which meant, even though Olivia had been right, Lucy should absolutely blame her.

Though she had only herself to blame for not listening when her sister had suggested Lucy pray about Graham. Lucy had been her usual self, thinking she could handle everything on her own, that she had everything under control. But this didn't feel under control.

This felt like riding a roller coaster with a broken seat harness.

Lucy didn't like being wrong. It was a strange occurrence for her.

It also wasn't like her to sit by herself, contemplating a turn of events she definitely hadn't seen coming. She should probably head back to the party. In a minute she would go dance with Danielle and her bridesmaids and have a good time.

After all, that was what she was: the good-time girl. Fun was her motto. She made it happen in her own life and others'. Only, today, the plan had completely backfired and she didn't know what to do about it.

A situation that made her very uncomfortable.

When footsteps sounded on the dock behind her, Lucy didn't turn. Her eyelids fell shut. It would be him. Noble Graham. Of course he would come check on her. Dread of their impending conversation settled like a brick in her stomach. He sat beside her, dangling his feet off the dock but not far enough to let the water touch his black dress shoes.

"You have great taste in shoes."

His quiet laugh answered her. "You okay?"

She felt his eyes on her and forced a smile. "Yep. You?"

He nodded.

She might as well get this over with. "About earlier—"

"Lucy—"

"Let me finish. I'm sorry. I was messing around and I shouldn't have." She really, really shouldn't have. "Trust me, if I could go back, I would." He had no idea how much she meant that.

"Stop apologizing, Lucy. It's not that big of a deal."

"Right. And that's why you've been avoiding me all night?"

He shrugged. "I just needed a little time to process. That's how my mind works."

She could see that.

"Despite the…ending, I had fun today, Duchess. The most fun I've had in a long time. You were right. I needed this."

She wanted to weep.

"I think today was good for me."

It wasn't today. It was me. I'm good for you. She resisted the desire to whack him across the back of the head and knock the thought into his brain. Instead, she settled for a huge, indulgent sigh.

"Anyway, let's just forget about…earlier."

Forgetting about it sounded like an impossible task. When Graham walked away, she'd have to dive into the water and fish her heart out from under the dock.

His response shouldn't sting, but it did. What had she expected him to say? *Lucy, I was wrong. Maybe there is room for someone else in my life. I just didn't realize it until you.*

Even if he was willing to move on, she wasn't crazy enough to think Graham would go for her in that way. They were too opposite. He was everything put together and she was everything falling apart. And she wouldn't change who she was, even for Graham.

But it would be nice to know that he at least had the potential to feel something for her. That truth stung, too. If Graham moved on with anyone, it would be with someone like Pearls. The woman he'd been dancing with had looked like a perfect fit for him.

"Did you meet someone?" She forced her gaze out to the water and fought the urge to tuck under his arm the way she had earlier today. It was as if she'd been pushed off a cliff. She'd gone from admitting nothing in regard to Graham to admitting everything. She needed to claw her way back up that mountain to her previous innocence. "I saw you dancing with—"

"Cherie? We've known each other since med school. She's a doctor down here now. She knew Brooke."

So he wasn't exactly asking the woman on a date. At least, not that Lucy knew of.

She *really* needed to get these newly discovered feelings under control. Graham had told her straight-out he didn't plan to date or marry. Therefore, this crush she was entertaining was not acceptable. And she *would* be deeming it a crush. It couldn't be more. She hadn't known Graham long enough for it to be more.

She could get over a crush. She could be logical about all of this.

Somehow she had to be. Because Graham was still married to his wife and always would be. Brooke's hold on his heart would go on forever. Lucy even understood it. If she'd lost someone like Graham had, that person would always have a piece of her. It made sense. But if there was any chance of sharing—if there was a possibility Graham could make room for Lucy and Brooke—she'd take that plunge. But Lucy knew there wasn't.

And she didn't stand a chance fighting a memory.

Chapter Eleven

"It still hurts." On Wednesday night, Mattie sat on the couch gripping a white blanket in her hands, lower lip protruding in an adorable pout.

Graham deposited a mug of warm milk on the coffee table in front of his daughter and held the back of his hand against her forehead. Still a low-grade fever.

"What hurts?"

"Everything, Daddy."

He sank to a sitting position on the coffee table, facing her. She might as well rip out his heart while she was at it. He might be a doctor, he might be able to deal with everyone else's medical problems, but when it came to Mattie, he was a mess.

He hated seeing her sick or in pain—just like he had Brooke. He knew Mattie had a virus that was going around. She had a temperature of 101, aches, pains and a runny nose. But even with that knowledge telling him that in a few days she would be fine, his feelings of helplessness continued to grow.

When Mattie had arrived at the clinic after school today, she'd looked a bit pale. At first, he'd thought it was a midweek thing. Sometimes she was exhausted on Wednesdays, especially going to full-day kindergarten. Plus, the previous weekend had been busy with him being gone all day Saturday and her sleeping over at his parents'.

He'd hoped she was just in need of a lazy movie night and pizza ordered in. But since that time a few hours ago, she'd spiked a fever and seemed to be heading rapidly downhill.

What was he going to do with her tomorrow? She wasn't showing signs of bouncing back overnight and he had to work. It wasn't as if he could cancel his patients for a day.

Graham got out his phone and texted his mom. She would watch Mattie—she always did. But that didn't make it any easier to see his girl sick.

"Do you want orange juice instead of milk? And we can put on *Frozen*." For the millionth time.

Her head swung back and forth.

"Do you want me to make soup?"

"Mommy's soup?"

When Mattie was younger, Graham had called chicken noodle soup "Mommy's soup," and the name had stuck. Not that he made it like Brooke used to. She'd made it from scratch—or at least partially homemade. She used to add dumplings and vegetables. Now Graham bought it premade. He wasn't even sure he had any in the cupboard.

"Let me check if we have some." He went into the kitchen and rummaged through the cupboards, sighing in relief when he found a package. After getting it started on the stove, he returned to the living room. He started the movie and then turned back to Mattie. "I've got the soup going. What else?"

When Mattie's eyes filled with moisture, Graham sank next to her on the couch, scooping her onto his lap. "Honey, I know you don't feel well. I'd do just about anything to make you feel better."

She toyed with her blanket. "I want Lucy."

Graham stiffened. He must have heard her wrong. Or

maybe she wanted one of her many stuffed animals, which she was constantly naming after people she knew.

"Is that the white tiger?"

Her small giggle warmed him. "No, Daddy. Ms. Lucy. Do you think she'd come over?"

No. No, he did not. Didn't he see enough of her? Since the weekend, he and Lucy had gone back to work, both adopting a "didn't happen" and "no big deal" approach about the kiss. It was working, but he didn't need to poke a sleeping bear.

"She's probably busy, honey."

"But you could check."

He could check. Hadn't he just said he'd do anything for Mattie? His daughter turned in his lap, looking up at him with those green eyes glimmering like mossy pools. "All right. I'll ask her, but if she can't, no getting upset. I'm sure she has other things going on." That thought gave him a bit of relief. Lucy was a fluttering social butterfly. She'd likely already have plans.

"But she loves me, Daddy."

He couldn't deny that. "You're right. She does." Heat sneaked under his shirt, and he tugged at his collar, fingers meeting the long-sleeved T-shirt he'd changed into after work. The way Lucy loved his daughter might be endearing, but that didn't mean it was a good idea to ask her over.

And he certainly didn't need to be a doctor to diagnose that the idea gave him a rapid pulse and shortness of breath.

Lucy propped her phone on the bathroom counter, putting it on speakerphone so she could continue talking with Bodie while she pulled her hair up. He'd called on Sunday and she hadn't answered, but today, she had.

They'd been on the phone for a while, and she had to admit, it was nice to talk to him again. She did like him.

She just wasn't sure anything could come of those feelings. Especially now that she'd figured out how she felt about Graham.

Knowing she couldn't have him felt like looking into a store window and seeing the most beautiful display, and then noticing the small sign hanging from it that said Not for Sale.

Was this what Liv was such a proponent of? This kind of achy feeling? Like being trampled by a horse? Lucy was so going to have a talk with her sister when she saw her tomorrow night.

"Let's go on a date this week."

She twisted her hair on top of her head. "How are we going to do that? You do recall that we live in different states. What are you going to do? Jump on a plane and fly down here?"

"Not a bad idea." His low voice did absolutely nothing to her stomach. So disappointing. She could totally go for a flip or jiggle of excitement. But maybe she needed to push past the lack of instant feelings. At least Bodie showed interest and pursued her. Something that would never happen with Graham.

"I meant over FaceTime. We could have dinner. I'll plan it. What do you say?"

Her cell showed a call from Graham, but Lucy ignored it. The man wasn't good for her. He made her heart all unhappy and hurting. This week at work, she'd made a conscious effort not to yank him into his office, slam the door and kiss him. Really kiss him this time. At least then they'd have something to fight about. Instead, they'd been perfectly nice to each other, leaving Lucy's gut churning with the desire for more. Not necessarily more kisses, though she'd take some of those, too, but more of Graham.

Since her realization about Graham at the wedding, Lucy had finally taken her sister's advice and started praying about him. About herself. About everything, really. What she should do after her job at the clinic ended. How to keep from going any further down sappy-crush lane. Her attempts at remembering to pray might be only slightly better than pathetic, but she was making an effort. That had to count for something, right?

"Lucy, you've pulled away since you moved. Give me another chance. Give us a chance."

What harm could a date with Bodie cause? It might get her mind off Graham for an evening. "Okay."

"Great. Friday night?"

"I haven't been on a Friday-night date in forever."

"Good. Because you should be dating me and nobody else." The mix of humor and determination in his voice made Lucy laugh.

After they hung up, she went into the bedroom of her small above-garage apartment and changed into plaid pajama pants and a long-sleeved T-shirt. She wanted to do nothing tonight. Maybe watch a movie. Eat popcorn for dinner. It seemed like that sort of a night.

When her phone beeped with a text, she hustled back into the bathroom and grabbed it from the counter.

I'm sorry to bother you. M is sick and she wants you. Any chance you're not busy?

Lucy's thumbs hovered over the keys. Seeing Graham probably wasn't in her best interests. Not with her still nursing this crush and daydreaming about kissing him in his office or an exam room too many times a day.

Saying no to Graham was one thing. But how could she say no to her Mattie girl?

When Lucy had entered Mattie's life, it wasn't on a temporary basis. At the time, it'd had nothing to do with Graham. Therefore, her relationship with the little girl should have nothing to do with Graham now.

He didn't affect her *that* much.

Right. Lucy had better not let her sister get hold of that one.

She showed up on his doorstep in typical Lucy style— pink-and-green plaid pajama pants, slippers that looked like knit ballet shoes and her hair piled in a mess on top of her head. It wasn't that cold, yet she looked ready to hunker down for a snowstorm the way she was bundled into her fleece jacket.

"Where is she? Is she okay?"

Graham swung the door farther open for her to come in. "She's fine. She's fighting something and she's emotional. You women seem to do that up-and-down thing when you're sick."

Lucy stepped into the house. "I have no idea what you're talking about. I'm solid as a rock. Haven't cried a day in my life."

"Right. *Even-keeled...* That's a word I would use to describe you."

Her eyes narrowed, lips pursed. His gaze fell to her mouth and stuck like Super Glue.

"I've missed you desperately in the few hours since work, Hollywood. I almost didn't know how I was going to go on without seeing you until morning."

Her sassy response had him fighting a smile, and his stress over Mattie not feeling well kicked down a notch. "I was just thinking the same about you, Duchess."

Graham swung the door shut and took Lucy's coat. She strode across the living room and dropped onto the couch, scooping Mattie's legs over her lap. "What's up, Matilda Grace? Is your dad driving you crazy? Are you faking being sick so that I would come over and rescue you from him?"

Mattie giggled and snuggled into Lucy.

"Dad, I'm hungry."

That was a good sign. Her medicine must be taking the edge off how she was feeling. "You just ate soup. What do you want now? Toast?"

"Chinese food. I want orange chicken."

Lucy held up a hand, which Mattie high-fived. "Best idea ever. Me, too. I'm starving." Both pairs of eyes swung to him, and those symptoms he'd had earlier started in again. They were both beautiful. Mattie's beauty stemmed from her serious nature, from the way she cared about people with a maturity far beyond her years—and the fact that she looked like a miniature Brooke. And Lucy's came from a combination of her effervescent personality, her big heart and the annoying fact that she was gorgeous. Even when she was wearing pajamas with her hair in a messy bun, the sight of her reached in and squeezed the air from his lungs.

What was he going to do with the two of them? They made a formidable team. And he was in trouble.

"Chinese food?" His voice cracked with all the maturity of a twelve-year-old boy. "I'll find the menu." And escape to the kitchen. He'd been right. Inviting Lucy over hadn't been a great idea.

Ever since the weekend, thinking of her in a professional way only was almost impossible.

Thinking of her in other ways—unfortunately—came more easily.

Graham got the take-out menu from the drawer. After asking Lucy what she wanted—which was to share and have a little of everything, big surprise—he called in the order.

He hung up and tossed the menu back in the drawer just as Mattie laughed at something Lucy said. His daughter didn't sound very sick right now. Was Lucy right? Was Mattie pretending not to feel well?

No way. Mattie might love Lucy, but she couldn't fake

a fever. It must be the meds—both the Lucy ones and the ibuprofen ones—making a difference.

When he headed back into the living room, Lucy was digging in the cupboard below the TV, half her body disappearing inside the space.

"Help yourself."

She scooted out, hitting her head on the way, then sat back and rubbed the spot, glaring at him.

"You okay?"

Her petulant look increased, lower lip protruding slightly. The desire to kiss away her pout washed over him. Until he remembered his daughter sitting on the couch watching the two of them. And the fact that he wasn't supposed to think of Lucy in that way.

"I'm fine. Mattie wants to play a game. She said they were in here."

"She said correctly."

Lucy reached into the cupboard and pulled a stack of games out, holding them on her lap. "Chutes and Ladders, Candy Land or Monopoly Junior?"

"Monopoly," Mattie answered with authority.

"That's my smart girl." Lucy shoved the other two back into the cupboard. They looked crooked, as though they might fall the next time he opened the door, but Graham resisted fixing them. He'd do it after she left.

Kind of like he'd vacuumed his car after their drive to San Antonio, just as he'd said he would.

Lucy set the game up on the coffee table and Graham turned the movie volume down, leaving it on in the background.

"Do we need to pick up the food?"

"I got it delivered."

"This town has delivery? Does someone show up on a horse?"

"We're not that small, Duchess." Although delivery was a rather new addition.

She laughed at her own joke, and his stomach did that annoying twist it did whenever Lucy was around. No medical terminology could describe it.

He sat on the floor on the other side of the coffee table, and they started the game. Mattie's attention span was a four out of ten at best, and she spent half the time dazed out and watching the movie, the other half being reminded to play. Though Lucy might have improved Mattie's mood, his daughter still wasn't feeling great.

Lucy, on the other hand, was a competitor. If he didn't watch it, she might own his actual house by the end of the night.

"Where'd you learn to play such a mean game of Monopoly?"

"My sister." Lucy took her turn and did not go to jail. "She's supercompetitive and loves to win. I always lost to her. You, on the other hand, are not as formidable an opponent."

He rolled the die. "I'm letting you win."

"I prefer to win my battles without assistance, as you probably already know."

True.

"But I also know that I am fairly and squarely knocking you on your behind, so no worries."

His mouth gave in to a grin. His daughter might be sick, but even with that, Graham knew he didn't want to be anywhere but where he was right now. Playing a game with Lucy and Mattie with a movie on in the background felt…right.

Had he been wrong all of this time? What if his theory on Brooke being the only love of his life was wrong? What if he could have that again? If it felt anywhere near as good as this, he would be a fool not to at least explore the possibility.

Graham would be lying if he didn't admit the kiss with Lucy had crossed his mind more than a few times this week.

But could that momentary lip-lock even be classified as

a kiss? He hadn't done much to take part in it. He'd moved in a bit, but he'd cut it off before anything could develop. If he was really going to kiss Lucy, he'd take his time. Thread fingers through her hair, which he imagined would be as soft as it looked, and pull her close. He'd savor the anticipation of his lips a moment from hers, the feel of her—

"Earth. To. Hollywood."

"What?"

"It's your turn."

"Oh." He laughed off his inattention, though the chuckle sounded more like a wounded duck. "Right. Sorry."

He took his turn and then Lucy started hers. He might be attracted to Lucy, but there was a difference between kissing her and pursuing a relationship. Even if he did decide to move past the idea that Brooke was his one and only love, he wouldn't let himself move in that direction with Lucy.

She was young. Too young for him. They were total opposites. And she was still his employee—an absolute no in his world.

Totally unprofessional.

Exactly like his thoughts a few seconds ago.

The doorbell rang, and Graham popped up. He grabbed his wallet from the side table and dug money out as he swung the door open.

"How much do I owe you?" He glanced up to see his in-laws standing on his front step.

"Nothing." Phillip attempted a smile, though it looked more like a grimace. "Were you expecting someone?"

"Food." The one syllable sounded strained. If Graham stepped outside and closed the door behind him, maybe the Wellings wouldn't see Lucy.

"Someone besides the owner of a yellow Volkswagen?" Phillip pointed with a thumb over his shoulder.

Then again, maybe not.

Chapter Twelve

By the scowls lining the Wellings' faces, they'd guessed the owner of the car.

"Come in." Graham forced himself to open the door wider. They glanced over his shoulder, their looks hardening.

He knew what they were seeing without having to look. Lucy and Mattie snuggled up under a white blanket, a game spread across the coffee table. An intimate scene Phillip and Belinda wouldn't appreciate.

The Wellings stepped inside, neither taking off their jackets, and the air in the room crackled with tension.

"Hi, Grandma and Grandpa!" Completely oblivious to the friction, Mattie waved from the couch. "Did you know I'm not feeling good so you came to see me like Lucy did?"

Lucy gave a small, tentative wave. The Wellings nodded regally at her, then asked about Mattie. Graham explained her symptoms, uncomfortable silence following.

Poor Lucy shifted on the couch, looking as if she wanted to crawl under the coffee table. Graham didn't blame her. In fact, he might join her.

"Mattie, why don't you show me your room?" She stood, but Mattie stayed under the blanket, confusion lining her features.

"How come? I thought we were going to eat."

"We will in a little bit." She picked Mattie up, and his daughter curled her arms and legs around Lucy. "Don't tell me what color your room is. I'm going to guess." Lucy walked past, eyes averted from him and the Wellings as she and Mattie disappeared up the stairs.

Another apology talk loomed in his future. Heat flared at the thought, spreading across Graham's skin. It shouldn't be this way. Why were Phillip and Belinda so cold to Lucy? Didn't they realize Mattie was in the room? She was a smart girl. Eventually she'd begin to question how her grandparents were acting.

He clamped his teeth together to keep from speaking his mind and motioned for them to move into the living room. They did so quietly, their unease radiating with each step.

The two of them sat on the chairs and Graham took the couch. He waited, not willing to make things easier for them. Not trusting himself to speak. Anger from the last time they'd treated Lucy this way rose up, stifling him.

"Graham." Phillip looked to his wife before continuing. "We heard a rumor yesterday, and we wanted to come straight to the source. We didn't want to believe it. But now that we're here…"

"We heard that you and Lucy went on a date to Danielle's wedding," Belinda continued. "The last time we talked to you about this, you said you weren't interested in dating Lucy."

He inhaled. Exhaled. Struggled for calm. "It wasn't a date."

"But you went to the wedding together, didn't you?"

"Yes, Belinda, we did. But the wedding was out of town. It was more about not driving two cars down than anything else." A half-truth. "And partly about Lucy wanting to do some sightseeing. It was completely innocent and not at all a date." At least the last part of that statement was true.

Why was Graham defending himself? He was thirty-one years old. He had a five-year-old daughter. He could make his own decisions. And what did they have against Lucy anyway?

"I think there's more to this than you're telling us." Belinda was the one carrying the conversation. Was all of this from her?

Graham turned to his father-in-law. "Phillip, are you part of this confrontation?"

He slowly nodded. "She was our only daughter."

An ache flickered in Graham's chest. "I know. And I loved her. I always will. But she's not here anymore. Believe me, if I could bring her back, I would."

"So you are dating Lucy." When Belinda piped up, Graham counted to five before answering.

"No. I'm not." His jaw hurt from clenching his teeth in order to keep from saying more. A full-out confrontation with the Wellings wasn't going to help the situation right now. If he got overly defensive, they'd assume he was dating Lucy no matter what he said.

"Graham, we just want you to be careful. This girl seems young—far too young to be a good influence on our granddaughter."

Graham didn't miss Phillip's emphasis on "our." As though the Wellings had part ownership or something. As though Graham wasn't the one ultimately in charge of Mattie.

"She probably sees that you're well-off, that you have a good profession. Perhaps she thinks she'll be set for life with you."

"Right." Belinda leaned forward, purse clutched in her hands as though a pickpocket might try to snatch it at any moment. "What do they call those young women who marry older men for money? Trophy wi—"

"Stop." Graham snapped the word out, cutting off Belinda. Yes, he was older than Lucy by seven years, but he didn't think that qualified him as *that* old. At least he hadn't before Belinda mentioned it. And the idea of Lucy going after his money—not that he was a millionaire or anything—was outrageous. He clamped down on the urge to laugh, knowing it definitely wouldn't help the moment. Lucy couldn't care less about all of that. She'd never think twice about his or anyone else's financial status.

If anyone should be accused of something, it was Phillip and Belinda. They were snobby to look down on Lucy or think she'd be after some free ride.

"Lucy's not trying to marry me." Strangely, no relief filled him at the statement. "And she's a great influence on Mattie." But she *was* young. The Wellings were right about that. Hadn't he thought the same thing just minutes ago? But young didn't mean immature. Lucy might always be looking for the next bit of adventure, but there wasn't anything wrong with that. Graham had come to appreciate that about her. He probably shouldn't mention to the Wellings that she'd deemed herself the Director of Fun in his life. He imagined that wouldn't go over well.

Belinda dug a tissue from her purse and dabbed under her eyelashes. Was she faking? Or really that upset? The Wellings had always been strong willed. When he and Brooke had first married, they'd had a few squabbles over holiday schedules, but eventually they'd worked things out. Still, those small disagreements didn't compare to this. He'd never seen them act this way during his marriage to Brooke or even after. The only point of contention since her death was that he refused to be on the board of her foundation.

Phillip leaned forward. "What about Brooke's money?"

Oh. He should have known there was more. Graham's head spun. "Brooke's money—" which had been given to *both* him and Brooke when they'd married "—is going to Mattie. We never touched it. It's in Mattie's trust fund. Her money for college."

Graham hadn't realized he or Lucy could be offended on so many levels in one conversation. Lucy would never take anything from Mattie. That the Wellings could even think it created a bitter taste in his mouth.

Did he know them at all?

"We're not okay with this." Phillip leaned forward, elbows resting on his knees.

Graham stifled a groan. He'd hoped the money discussion would end their doubts.

"You tell us you're not dating her, but not only do we hear you went to a wedding with her, we come over and find her at your house." Phillip's eyebrows thundered together. "In her pajamas, of all things." He spread his hands. "How do you think this looks to us?"

Graham's defense caved a bit. "It probably doesn't look good. But I don't know how many ways to tell you that you're jumping to conclusions."

"If we're jumping to conclusions now, it's only because we see what's happening and you don't," Phillip stated.

Belinda sniffled. "We want you to stay away from her. We don't believe she's right for you. And if you date her… we're not going to stay around to watch her break both of your hearts."

His world crashed down around him. "What are you saying?"

Belinda glanced to Phillip before continuing. "We're saying it's her or us."

How could they even voice such a thing?

Graham couldn't sit in the same room with them. The temptation to walk out the front door of his own house and escape this nightmare was strong. If the girls weren't upstairs—and hopefully not hearing any of this conversation—he'd consider it. He popped up from the couch and paced behind it.

He wasn't dating Lucy and he didn't plan to, but the Wellings had no business getting involved in his life like this. They were out of line and being completely outrageous. He should tell them to get out of his house right this instant…that they didn't have any right.

But then what? They'd walk out and Mattie would never see them again?

Anger sank into despair. Graham couldn't let that happen. Losing Brooke had been hard enough. Knowing he should have been able to save her but couldn't had broken something inside of him.

He'd never be able to live with himself knowing he could have stopped Phillip and Belinda from walking out of Mattie's life.

Yes, they were being completely irrational. Judgmental. Inconsiderate. Untrusting.

The list could go on for days.

But a check in his gut told him none of that mattered. Because they were Mattie's grandparents. Despite the way they were acting right now, they loved Mattie dearly. And she loved them back. Which meant he needed to cave to them.

"I'm not going to date Lucy." His voice was low, broken. "I don't know how many ways to say the same thing. You're just going to have to trust me." If he'd already made the decision on his own earlier, why did saying the words now make him feel as though he had a collapsed lung?

At this point, it didn't matter what he felt. Another person wouldn't be ripped from Mattie's life because of him.

Including Lucy.

"I won't date her, but she is going to be in Mattie's life. She's good for Mattie. If you can't see that, then I don't know what to tell you." Standing up for her felt like a small victory, and the sag in his shoulders straightened a little.

The Wellings exchanged a look, as though they were deciding how far to push. Phillip spoke. "How long will this Lucy be working for you?"

Graham ignored the "this" before "Lucy." He had to pick his battles.

"Another two and a half weeks."

The couple communicated with each other again without saying a word. Then Phillip nodded. "Okay. Deal. We'd prefer no contact at all, but since that's not an option, we'll concede to her being in Mattie's life."

Deal.

Graham felt nauseated, as though he'd just made a shady business agreement in a back alley. He half expected Phillip to offer him a handshake over it. Thankfully he didn't.

The Wellings showed themselves out, and Graham walked around and dropped onto the couch, a flood of feelings coursing through him. Anger. Bitterness.

Disappointment.

Before he could analyze that last one, a knock sounded at the door. He grabbed his wallet from the coffee table and went to open it. No surprises greeted him this time. After paying, he called upstairs. The girls came down—Mattie with more excitement than Lucy.

"Where are Grandpa and Grandma?"

"They had to go."

Hurt registered in Mattie's wilting shoulders. Though Graham still felt sickened by the conversation he'd just had with the Wellings, seeing Mattie's response to their quick departure told him he'd done what he needed to do in order to protect her from anything worse in the future.

She peered up at him. "Are we eating in the living room?"

He'd let her eat hanging from the ceiling if that was what she wanted. "Why not?"

"I'll get the plates." Mattie ran into the kitchen, her momentary upset quickly forgotten.

Lucy shoved a jittery hand through her hair, causing a few strands to fall from the bun on top of her head. "I'm completely confused by her. One moment she's running across her room. The next she's crashed in her bed."

"It's the medicine."

"She introduced me to all of her stuffies. There's even one named after me. And her coloring pages are amazing. So detailed for her age. Not that I know what a typical five-year-old draws like, but of course Mattie would do anything better than anyone else. At least, in my opinion."

"Mine, too." Graham rested a hand on her arm to stop her nervous chatter. "It's going to be okay, Lucy."

Worried blue eyes pierced him. "Is it? Do they want me to stay away from Mattie?"

Yes. "I told them that's not an option. You're good for her." *And me.*

"Okay." Lucy's quiet acceptance didn't erase her sad look. Mattie came back into the living room with plates and silverware, and he resisted smoothing the crease pulling at Lucy's mouth.

"You okay?"

"Yep." She crossed her arms, causing his hand to drop from her skin. "You?"

No. He wasn't. Lucy was hurt and he felt as though he'd been to battle. He wanted to tuck her into his arms, kiss the top of her head and make her sad go away.

Exactly what he'd just said he wouldn't do. He had the sinking feeling that all of his excuses for not being interested in Lucy were simply that.

But what could he do about that now? With the Wellings so upset, Graham couldn't develop feelings for Lucy. Mattie would lose two people she loved from her life if he did.

It was best if he kept his thoughts about Lucy centered on friendship and their mutual love for Mattie.

Surely that would be safe.

But even with that plan in mind, he couldn't shake the thought that he'd just made a trade he'd come to regret… his happiness for Mattie's.

Lucy dished a second helping of kung pao chicken and fried rice, then dumped on a packet of soy sauce. She expected a remark from Graham about all of the salt intake, but his commentary had been sadly missing from the evening ever since his in-laws had shown up. Lucy was torn between asking what had happened and not wanting to know.

She waved a hand in front of him. "You still there?" They were sitting on the floor, their plates on the coffee table. A few minutes ago, Mattie had finished a small helping and climbed onto the couch behind Lucy.

Graham had checked her forehead, stated that her fever was back, then returned to eating.

Lucy's back was against the couch, and she could feel Mattie's fingers holding on to her shirt with a slight grip. Endearing little gesture.

"I'm still here."

"You want to talk about it?"

"Nope." Graham tempered his comment with a half-smile. "Tell me a story. Something about you I don't know."

Going home would be a better option. The way this man directed her heartstrings was getting pathetic. She wanted to make him smile and laugh. She wanted her Graham back. Whatever Brooke's parents had said to him certainly hadn't gone well.

"I'll say three things. Two true. One made up. You guess which one isn't true."

"Okay." Graham studied her with amusement, and she fought the desire to lean across the table and give him a smacking kiss. Happy. Angry. Sad. The man looked good wearing any emotion.

Good thing she had this *crush* of hers under control.

"I've jumped out of an airplane. I've been to Europe. I've been hunting."

He set his plate to the side and wiped his mouth with a napkin. "That's easy. You've never been hunting."

"Ha! I have been hunting. I haven't jumped out of a plane."

"No way."

"Yes way." Lucy propped a hand under her chin. "Would this face lie?"

Graham chuckled, and no matter who won the game, Lucy already had her victory in the bag.

"What kind of hunting? I'm not sure I believe this scenario. Does this involve an old boyfriend?"

"No." She scoffed. "I wouldn't go hunting for a boy. In junior high, my friend wanted to go with her dad. We were joined at the hip and did everything together, so we both went. I didn't shoot anything." She raised a finger. "But I did go."

"Okay, I believe you."

"You're up, Hollywood."

"Hang on. I'm thinking." He took his time, closing food containers and stacking dishes. Lucy tapped her fingers on the coffee table. She rolled her neck. She could probably teach a dance class and get back before he came up with anything.

Finally Graham stopped cleaning up everything on the coffee table. "I've delivered a baby. I've always lived in Texas. I've never broken a bone."

"I think, despite your cautious nature, that you've definitely broken a bone."

"Actually, I never have."

"What? That doesn't make sense, then, because I'm pretty sure you've always lived in Texas, and you're a doctor, so you must have delivered a baby at some point in your career."

"Technically I haven't always lived in Texas." He looked like a kid who'd just got away with an extra dessert. "One summer I spent a month with my cousin in Idaho."

"That's practically cheating." Not that she cared with that grin claiming his mouth. She loved seeing him happy after whatever had happened with his in-laws. "Next you'll tell me the baby you delivered was Mattie. I'm not sure that counts, either."

His smile fell. "What? No, of course not. Brooke was considered high risk with cystic fibrosis. The two of them had a team of doctors far more qualified than me for Mattie's delivery."

"Oh." Guess that made sense. Although, the way Graham talked…

"Spill, Duchess. I can tell you're thinking something."

Lucy toyed with the edges of the throw she had over her lap. "You're a great doctor, Graham. You do know that, right? I would trust you with my life."

He busied himself collecting their silverware. "How do you know? You're working in the front office, not in on the appointments."

Could he seriously doubt himself?

"I hear plenty." Lucy shrugged. "I know your patients love you, that they trust you and keep coming back."

"I do my best, but I'm still human. Sometimes I wonder…"

"What?"

"Nothing." He shook his head, then motioned to the couch behind Lucy. She glanced over her shoulder to find Mattie asleep, lashes grazing her cheeks, pink skin giving hints of the fever within. She still had one hand near Lucy, as if she'd held on until sleep won.

Lucy turned back to Graham. "I kind of have a thing for her."

"I've noticed." His gaze roamed her face. "It's nice. Thank you. And thanks for coming over. She was a mess before you got here."

Lucy knew the feeling. A bit like she felt now. "You're welcome. Graham, are you sure the Wellings don't want me to stay away from Mattie?" Ever since she'd been upstairs with Mattie, the thought had been clanging around in her head. She'd tried to ignore it. She'd tried to believe what Graham had told her earlier when she came downstairs, but she really needed to know the truth.

If she couldn't see Mattie anymore, Lucy would need someone to sew her shredded heart back together. It was bad enough she harbored these feelings for Graham. Not having either of them in her life might do her in.

"They aren't allowed to think that. I told them you were good for Mattie and that you would be in her life."

Though he'd conveniently avoided answering what the Wellings thought, Lucy accepted his reply. Relief that she wasn't going to lose Mattie rolled down her spine, and she stretched back against the couch before realizing there must be more. "So if it wasn't that, then…"

"I really don't want to talk about it."

"It must have something to do with me. They barely acknowledged my presence." Lucy felt as though she were poking a hornet's nest, but she couldn't stop herself.

"They just love their daughter, and the thought of me moving on with anyone is hurting them."

Moving on. The thing Graham never planned to do. "So did you tell them—"

"Yes, I did." He looked everywhere but at her, then popped up and grabbed items from the coffee table. "I told them. I mean, of course we know we're not together, that our relationship is built around Mattie and work."

Lucy's heart felt squeezed in a massive fist. What had she expected? She'd hoped she could get through the evening by concentrating on Mattie. She'd thought she could ignore her feelings for Graham, but tonight had made her do anything but. Being with them, all cozy and tucked in— even with Mattie sick—felt right.

Her feelings were going beyond crush into crushing.

Lucy should be thankful that the Wellings had appeared unexpectedly tonight. They'd saved her some heartache. Because despite the fact that Graham must have stood up for her and defended her relationship with Mattie, Lucy knew the truth.

She didn't fit. Not in the Wellings' world, and not with Graham and Mattie.

Chapter Thirteen

During the hour Mattie had been at dance class, Graham had grabbed a coffee and done their grocery shopping for the week. And Lucy thought he never did anything fun.

Thankfully, his little girl had started feeling better late yesterday. Graham had tried to talk Mattie out of dance this morning, telling her she might be a bit weak from having a fever the past few days, but she'd adamantly refused to miss it. He'd let Lucy know when he'd dropped Mattie off this morning that she might not make it through the whole class.

After the week they'd had, Graham wouldn't mind doing nothing besides church for the rest of the weekend. But that wasn't an option.

The last thing he wanted to do was spend his Saturday night with the Wellings after their confrontation on Wednesday. But that was exactly what he had to do. Once a year, they hosted a gala to raise funds for Brooke's charity. All of their rich friends attended, and last year Graham had spent the evening feeling alone in the middle of a crowd. This year would be no different. It was the one thing he agreed to attend for the charity, and the Wellings would never understand his not being there.

His phone rang just as he got out of the car. He shut the door and answered his cell. "Hey, Dad."

"Graham, I hate to be the bearer of bad news…"

"What's wrong?" His mind raced with all kinds of bad scenarios.

"Mom's sick. She has a fever. Her eyes are glassed over and she's going at quarter speed."

"From Mattie." He felt horrible. "I'm sorry, Dad. If she hadn't taken care of Mattie, then she wouldn't—"

"Enough. Your mother will be fine. She loves taking care of Mattie, sick or not. I'm calling because you'd wanted me to go with you tonight, but Mom can't watch Mattie. I can stay home and watch her."

Graham had asked his dad to go with him a few weeks ago, but as the gala drew near, the importance of his father being there was growing. "Don't make me handle all of those people on my own." Especially the Wellings. Since Graham had moved back to Fredericksburg, Dad had become one of his closest friends. Graham wanted a support person there tonight. Someone to keep him from telling the Wellings what he really wanted to say. Someone wise and calm like his father. Mattie's relationship with her grandparents had to come first. No matter what other things Phillip and Belinda accused Graham of.

"I'm fine going, but what are you going to do about Mattie? I already checked with your sisters before I called you and neither of them can watch her."

Graham sighed. He didn't even want to go tonight, and now he had to stick Mattie with a sitter. "I'll find someone." They hung up, and Graham thumbed through the contact list on his phone.

He rarely had to hire anyone with family in town, but there were a few high school girls he could check with. He found the first number and pressed Send. On the fourth ring, a sleepy voice answered.

"Hey, Kieta, this is Graham Redmond. I'm sorry if I woke you up. I'm looking for a babysitter for tonight for Mattie. I know it's late notice—"

"I'm sorry, Dr. Redmond, but there's a big party tonight. You'll probably have a hard time finding someone."

Perfect. "Okay, thanks for letting me know." They hung up, and Graham rubbed the stress from his eyes. He could call the Wellings and tell them he couldn't find a sitter, but knowing them, they'd call a service and send someone to his door.

If he wasn't concerned about sending their currently tumultuous relationship into further turmoil, he'd just cancel for tonight. Nothing would make him happier right now.

"Dad!" Mattie skipped across the sidewalk to him. "Class is over. What are you doing?" He scooped her up, burying his nose in her peach-shampoo hair. After a short hug, Mattie squirmed, forcing him to set her down. She propped her hands on her hips and tapped one toe, a move that reminded him of Lucy. The woman was definitely rubbing off on his daughter.

"What's going on, Daddy? Your face looks all scrunchy."

He wrinkled his nose. "Thanks for the compliment." Her little giggle would never get old. "How did class go? Did you make it all the way through?"

"Of course. Why wouldn't I?"

Kids. They always bounced back faster than adults. "No reason."

"We had to practice for the recital. I can't miss class, Daddy. It's very important. We got to see the dresses today, and they're beautiful." Mattie stretched out the word and spun in a circle, arms wide.

"What recital?"

"The spring recital," Lucy answered, approaching behind Mattie. "It's in two weeks. Mattie's in two dances."

"I didn't know anything about it."

Lucy was wearing her typical leggings and long, fitted T-shirt, though today her hair was in a braid sneaking over her shoulder. She wore pink Converse shoes and she looked…adorable. But not in a little-girl way. Nope. She just looked like beautiful, carefree Lucy.

"At first I didn't tell you about it because I thought you'd say no."

He dropped a hand to his chest in mock offense. "Me? That's crazy." When she smiled, his gaze landed on her lips. He scrambled to distract himself. "Doesn't Mattie need a dress or outfit?"

"Yep."

"Where do we get it?"

"You don't. We order way in advance, and since you were tentative about dance in the beginning—"

"Ha. That's a nice way of putting it."

The skin surrounding her eyes crinkled. "I ordered her stuff without telling you so that she'd have it for recital. I knew we needed to get it right away in order for her to have it in time."

"And so you did it without my knowledge." When Graham had first met Lucy, this conversation would have irked him. Now he just felt relieved. She'd gone behind his back and taken care of everything so that his little girl would have what she needed. "Thank you for doing that."

Lucy visibly relaxed. "You're welcome."

"How much do I owe you?"

"We'll figure it out." She waved a hand. "It's not that big of a deal."

Mattie tugged on his arm. "Daddy, I heard Mrs. Knoll say the dresses were fifty dollars."

He leveled Lucy a look. "I'm paying for the dress."

"That's fine. I wasn't saying you couldn't."

"Okay, good." The conversation stalled. He wanted to say something more about the other night, but words failed him. After Lucy left Wednesday, Graham had fought the feeling that he'd made an even bigger mess out of everything. Not that he knew how to fix any of it.

He was more attracted and more drawn to Lucy with

each passing day, but with Phillip and Belinda threatening to walk out of Mattie's life if he dated her, the woman was off-limits.

"I'm going to my grandparents' house tonight, Ms. Lucy." Mattie did a small dance of excitement.

"That's great, Mattie Grace."

"Actually, they can't watch you tonight, Mattie. You're going to have a sitter."

Her lower lip protruded. "I don't want a sitter."

"I don't want you to have one either, but that's the way it has to happen."

Lucy stepped closer. "Why? What's the deal?"

"Nothing." Graham really, really didn't want to talk about any of this with Lucy. "Come on, Mattie. Let's go."

"Why can't Ms. Lucy watch me tonight?" His sweet little girl crossed her arms and huffed. Actually huffed. Next she'd probably throw herself down on the ground and have one of the fits she'd skipped out on during the first five years of her life.

"Because I'm sure Lucy has plans. Maybe with her sister. Or maybe she even has a…date." The word tasted weird on his tongue, then bowled him right over. Here he was, analyzing whether his feelings for Lucy were changing, and she might be dating someone. She might not think of him as anything more than old. And lame.

Those were two very real possibilities.

"Had a date last night."

That answered that question. The disappointment roaring through him couldn't be a good sign.

"But not tonight." Lucy bent to Mattie's level. "And I think a girls' night is a great idea. We can do our nails, put on makeup—"

"She's not wearing makeup."

She winked at Mattie, then faced Graham. "Come on, Hollywood. You've been doing so much better with just letting me do what I want. A little makeup that washes right off isn't going to hurt."

"I didn't even agree to you watching her. It's out of the question."

Her eyes narrowed. "Why? Don't you trust me?"

"Of course I trust you. It's just, besides the fact that you already do too much for Mattie, this thing tonight… It's for Brooke's charity."

"That's great!"

"With the Wellings."

"Oh." Hurt flashed, but after one look at Mattie, she squared her shoulders. "Well, are they coming to your house before?"

"No."

"Then what time should I be there?"

Only ten minutes behind schedule, Lucy knocked on Graham and Mattie's front door. It had taken her some time this morning to convince Graham that not only would she watch Mattie tonight, but that if he offered to pay her, it would signal the end of their friendship for eternity.

While it was rather stinky to be just the babysitter, at least Lucy got to hang with her favorite little girl. And in lieu of Graham declaring he couldn't live without her, she would take a girls' night with a five-year-old.

"Hey, it's getting cold out here," she yelled at the still-closed front door. And by cold, she meant sixty degrees and drizzling rain. Yikes. She'd grown way too accustomed to the warm Texas weather.

The door flew open. "It is not cold. Aren't you supposed to be used to snow and freezing weather, Colorado girl?"

Graham was wearing a black tux with a crisp white shirt, his bow tie undone and hanging around his neck. *Good night.* Lucy was going to need at least five minutes before she could speak coherently.

His head tilted. "Why are you still standing out there? Quick—get in out of the cold."

"Ha." She managed a strangled response to his sarcasm— her *ha* sounding a little pirate-y and more like a *har-har*. She moved past him, catching a whiff of his cologne as she did. Her eyelids slid shut. She'd got used to how he smelled, being around him so much, but tonight, combined with the tux, *ai yai yai*.

"Where's Mattie?" *Please, go get Mattie. I need her to stop me from ruining everything between us by declaring my undying devotion to your cologne.*

"She's upstairs." Graham faced the mirror above the small entry table and started tying his bow tie. What man knew how to tie one of those without help? He looked movie-premiere good, and he was headed out to spend the evening in a world Lucy didn't belong in.

Good times on a Saturday night.

At least she'd been able to drop that line earlier about her date with Bodie last night. It wasn't so much that she'd wanted to gauge Graham's response—though that part had been nice—but more that she'd wanted him to know. Because, every so often, she wondered if Graham felt something between them, too. And she just wanted to be honest that she was dating other people. One other person. On one date. Over FaceTime.

Oh, maybe she shouldn't have said anything at all.

But Bodie had been an amazing date, even over a computer screen. He'd had flowers and dinner delivered to her door.

"What's going on with you tonight?" Graham had turned from the mirror and was studying her. "I told you I could have found a sitter. Mattie's not—"

"You ordering us pizza?"

He nodded.

"Then we're good. In fact, the sooner you go, the better. We have girl things to do." She set the bag she'd brought along on the coffee table. It included makeup—despite Graham's protests—movies, nail polish and hair chalk. Lucy didn't think she was brave enough to use that last one on Mattie even though it would wash right out. Graham would lose his mind. On second thought, it might be kind of fun if he saw Mattie in the morning with bright-colored streaks in her hair and thought it was permanent.

"What's in there?"

She tossed a look over her shoulder. "Nothing you need to know about."

Graham followed her into the living room, looking a bit like a lost puppy. "I don't want to go."

Oh, honey. Lucy stepped toward him. "I know things have been tough between you guys, pretty much because of me—"

"That's not true."

She raised an eyebrow and continued. "But you're doing this for Brooke, not them. And for Mattie. You can do it."

He drank her in, and her knees just about went into retirement right then and there. Finally, he sighed and scrubbed a hand across the back of his neck. "You're right."

"Always."

"Right." His tone was low and wry and made her stomach take a roller-coaster ride. "Always." His smile made an appearance. Combined with the tux, the woodsy cologne and the man, she needed to sit down.

She sank to the couch. "So, exciting date for tonight?"

"Yep."

The comment had been meant as a joke, something to get her mind off her close proximity to Graham, but it had backfired big-time. Had he changed his mind about dating? What had happened? Was he really going out with—

"My dad."

Oh. Oh. Oh. Sweet Graham. Lucy loved that he'd go to his father for support. She also loved that she wasn't watching Mattie while Graham went on a date with another woman. "Sounds like a good person to help you survive tonight." In more ways than one. She assumed tonight would be hard for him with thoughts of Brooke bombarding him throughout the evening.

"Hi, Ms. Lucy!" Mattie flew down the stairs and slid across the living room floor in her socks, joining Lucy on the couch.

"Someone's definitely all the way better."

"She's been bouncing off the walls all day. Very unMattie-like. I think—" Graham slid his hands into his pants pockets "—she might be a little excited for tonight."

Couch cushions jiggled as Mattie agreed.

"But she also knows she's going to bed at the normal time."

The girl's lower lip slipped into a pout before she switched back to excitement. "Are we going to do nails?"

"As soon as your dad gets out of here."

Mattie popped up from the couch and started shoving Graham toward the door.

"Hey!" His hands rose in the air. "I'm going. Hang on. I have to grab my keys and wallet." He picked them up from the small entry table. "Pizza should be here soon. It's already paid for. And if anything goes wrong, Lucy, just call me—"

"We got it." Mattie gave him one more shove, and Graham opened the front door. "Emergency numbers are on the fridge. We're good, Dad. Later."

"Don't I at least get a kiss?"

Graham leaned down, and Mattie bestowed a smacking smooch on his cheek.

How disappointing. For a second there, Lucy had hoped he'd been talking to her.

Chapter Fourteen

Graham put the key in the lock of his front door, then let his head fall silently to rest on the cool wood. The night had gone much as he'd expected—a lot of schmoozing with people he barely knew. But it had also had some unexpected parts—like the ache that had radiated in his chest all night. Not acid reflux or any other diagnosable illness. Nope. This had been a churning mixture of guilt and loneliness. Because on a night when he should have been thinking about Brooke—and he had, of course—he'd been missing Lucy.

Lucy.

The woman who was in his house right now because she was willing to watch his daughter, willing to walk right into their lives and make an impact in places he didn't remember feeling before.

He was in trouble. For the first time since Brooke, he knew he wanted to move on…and he couldn't. The Wellings made that impossible. Because no matter what Graham selfishly wanted—to walk into his house and sink into kissing Lucy—he wouldn't do that to Mattie.

She'd already lost her mom. She wouldn't lose a relationship with her grandparents because of him.

He gave in to a pathetic sigh before standing upright and turning the key in the lock. Enough wallowing. He'd just discovered—or been willing to admit—these feelings for Lucy. Maybe they weren't that strong. Maybe she didn't reciprocate them and he was frustrated over nothing. After all, she'd had a date last night.

Who had she gone out with? Graham saw her every day of the week between work, dance and church, and he'd never seen her with a guy who looked like a boyfriend.

He stepped into the house.

"Hey." A rumpled Lucy sat up from where she'd been lounging on the couch. "That was a quiet entrance. I was hoping for a blasting boom box being held over your head from the front yard or a lawn-mower ride or something."

Graham dug the stuff from his pockets, depositing it on the front table. "I take it you've been watching '80s movies all night?"

"Since Mattie went to bed."

"You couldn't have fit too many in."

"Just two. But I've seen them all."

"Of course."

He loosened his tie and walked over, dropping into one of the chairs across from the couch.

"Was it that bad?"

He shrugged. "I'd rather have been here."

"Well, that's a given. I am extremely delightful to be around."

Graham rubbed his temples, the slightest curve touching his mouth. "I feel like you've told me that exact thing before."

"Possible, because it's true." Lucy stood and started folding the blanket.

"You don't need to do that."

She ignored him, continuing to tidy up. He should get out of the chair and help her, but he didn't trust himself to be anywhere near her right now.

He still couldn't believe he'd missed her tonight, couldn't believe these feelings had sneaked up on him. Yes, he'd known he was attracted to her. The thought of dating her had crossed his mind before, but he'd really hoped their relationship could revolve around Mattie and stay at friendship level. His reasons for not developing feelings for Lucy—her age, their opposite personalities, the fact that she still worked for him—were all legit.

They just weren't working.

He'd been blind, and because of the Wellings, he needed to figure out how to remain that way.

"Okay, I'm going to go."

Graham stayed where he was. "Thank you for tonight."

"Of course. Like I said before, it's not a problem."

She walked toward him, sitting on the armrest of his chair. Too close. She smelled so good, he just wanted to drink in everything about her. The way her braid fell over one shoulder as she leaned forward, the concerned look pulling on the mouth that could hold his attention for days.

Her hand rested on his forehead. "No fever. Thought maybe you were coming down with what Mattie had."

"I'm fine."

"You're not. You're sad, and I don't like it." She pointed to herself. "Director of Fun, remember?"

"How could I forget?"

"Are you sure you don't have a temp?"

Graham caught her hand on the way to his forehead again and placed a kiss on the inside of her wrist. He shouldn't have, but he hadn't been able to resist. She sucked in a breath and held very still.

After a few seconds, she slid from the chair and stood. "I—"

"You can't fix this, Lucy. It's okay. I'll be okay."

"At least one of us will be." And then she was gone.

"I have a problem."

"What's wrong?" Olivia sounded as if she'd been asleep,

and Lucy winced when she checked the time above her rearview mirror.

"I'm sorry. I didn't even realize how late it was. I forget Cash gets up so early—"

"Cash wants to know where you're stranded. He says he'll be right there."

"I'm fine. Not stranded. Boy trouble."

"Oh."

Lucy heard Olivia explain to Cash that nothing was wrong, some shuffling, then a door open and close.

"Okay, I'm out of the room. What's going on?"

"I want him to be happy."

"Sounds like a crime to me. Of course, I was asleep, so there's a chance I'm not following you."

"He kissed my wrist."

"Was he aiming for your mouth?"

"You are seriously snarky when you get woken up."

Olivia's sigh echoed over the phone. "Sorry. I'll try for silent, but I'm going to need more details. And to know which guy we're talking about."

"There's only one guy."

"Not true. Didn't you just go on a date with Bodie last night?"

Yes. She had. But Lucy would have to tell Bodie that couldn't happen again. Even if Graham didn't reciprocate her feelings, she couldn't continue to date Bodie when she was falling for someone else.

"Graham. When he got back from his dinner-fundraiser thing tonight, he was so sad, Liv."

"I'm sorry."

"Me, too. And I just wanted him to be happy. And then it hit me after I got into the car. Maybe he can be, but just not with me. His in-laws are like a big brick wall between us. I don't know what their deal is, exactly. I only know it can never happen."

"Never say never."

Lucy fought the tears that surfaced without permission. "You know how optimistic I am, but it's not even remotely possible. They don't like me. I'm not good enough for them, their world, their granddaughter…or Graham."

"Has anyone said that to you?"

"Not in words." Lucy sniffled. But sometimes words weren't necessary.

"I am obviously not in agreement with that thinking, but go on."

"I realized if Graham's willing to give up the *I'm never getting married again* thing, maybe he could move on with someone else. He could have a future with someone the Wellings approve of. And then my heart was breaking, because I knew I wanted that happiness for him…even if it's not with me."

"Oh, Lulu. It sounds like you really care about him. Welcome to maturity."

"Maturity stinks."

"Yep. It can. But sometimes it works out in the end."

"I'm not sure this story is going to end that way, Liv. This isn't a fairy tale."

Silence met her, and she swiped at the tear that managed to escape. Lucy wasn't much of a crier. She was going to add this to her list of things to complain about after growing touchy-feely feelings for someone. Why in the world was her sister such a big proponent of this stuff?

"Lulu, you're right. It might not work out. Not everything does. I can only tell you I'll be praying about all of this. And will you do me a favor?"

Strange time to be asking for things. "What is it?"

"This stuff with Graham's in-laws has been wounding for you." Lucy wanted to interrupt and deny it, but Olivia didn't give her a chance. "Just don't forget God created you to be exactly who you are for a reason. How God views you—how much He adores you—that's a truth you should believe."

At the reminder, peace trickled through Lucy. "Good thing I have a wise older sister to take my midnight phone calls."

"If I'm wise, which I doubt, it's only because I've learned from making many, many mistakes. You, my dear sister, are now the lovely recipient of the knowledge gained from my life lessons."

Despite feeling as though she'd lost her heart somewhere back at Graham's house, Lucy's amusement grew. "First I was almost in tears. Now I'm laughing. Go back to bed, pregnant mama. Thanks for talking me through this."

"Anytime."

"Except maybe not at two in the morning."

"Right. Maybe not then."

"Hurry up, Dad!" Two weeks later, Graham found himself being dragged across the high school parking lot with superhuman strength by a five-year-old girl who refused to be anything less than early for her first dance recital.

"We're on time, I promise." His reassurances were met by silence. "Are you nervous about tonight, Mattie? It's okay if you feel scared and excited at the same time."

She stopped walking and looked at him, bright eyes accentuated behind red glasses. "My stomach hurts."

"That's nerves, honey, and they aren't a bad thing. Sometimes they can be from excitement, too. I know you're going to do great. And no matter what happens, I'll think you're amazing."

She gave him an exasperated look, and he tried his best not to smile. "You have to, Daddy. You don't count."

"Uh, thank you?"

She giggled, grabbed his hand again and took off for the doors. "All of this talking is making us late."

Ten minutes later, they'd found Mattie's group in a classroom staging area where the girls would stay before and after their part of the performance. Coloring books and crayons were spread out on the floor, along with a handful of girls in bright blue tutus. Mattie fit right in, dropping to the ground and chatting with one of the little girls from her class.

"When did she grow up?"

Lucy appeared beside him. "In the last week."

"That's what I was thinking."

They shared a grin.

"Do you need me to stay in here with her?"

"Nope. Go enjoy the show. I have a few mom volunteers who'll be back here helping keep the girls entertained and their hair perfect while we wait for our performances."

"Hair?" Graham panicked. "I didn't do Mattie's hair a certain way. I didn't even know that was a thing."

"Chill." Lucy shook her head, amusement evident. "I've got everything she needs. Curling iron, ginormous bow, more bobby pins than necessary. I'm prepared."

"Okay." He let out a jagged breath.

"Nervous, are we?"

"Me?" He attempted a chuckle but it came out as a wheeze. "No. Maybe." He tugged Lucy away from the girls. "What if she forgets her steps? Or gets stage fright? Are you sure she's ready? The rest of the girls have been in class all year. Mattie's only been going for two months. I don't want her to feel embarrassed if something goes wrong."

"She'll be fine. Relax. I've been praying over this night for her. I think it's a big step for our serious little girl. She's so excited, and I think she's going to do great."

Our little girl.

He wanted to kiss her. Right there, in the middle of a bunch of five- and six-year-olds, he wanted to let his lips find Lucy's and never let her go.

"Graham, there you are!" his mom called from over his shoulder, and then she was next to him. Jabbering to Lucy.

Hugging her. Short blond hair dancing around her chin with excitement.

"I'm Nancy Redmond. It's so nice to finally meet you, Lucy. We've heard so much about you from Mattie and Graham. You'll have to come over for lunch on a Sunday so we can get to know you better."

Since his parents attended a different church than he and Mattie did, his mom and dad had never met Lucy. Much to his mother's dismay. Sounded as if she planned to make up for lost time.

Lucy nodded as his mom continued talking, unable to get a word in.

"I'm just so excited to see Mattie dance. Oh, Mattie— hi, love bug!" Like a butterfly flitting from one flower to another, his mom moved to hug Mattie.

"Gary Redmond." Graham's father introduced himself, shaking Lucy's hand. "I might not show it in the same way as my wife, but I'm equally excited to meet you." Graham and his father shared a number of similarities. Both had dark hair, though his dad's had started peppering with gray over the past few years. Their build was also alike. And their minds... By the way his dad currently studied him, Graham feared his feelings for Lucy were an open book. Hopefully the Wellings wouldn't have their magnifying glasses out tonight.

Dad turned back to Lucy. "Thanks for all you've done for Mattie."

"Of course."

They continued talking, and Graham's neck heated, warmth creeping onto his cheeks. He needed to get out of this room. Lucy meeting his parents was giving him false hope that she would fit with his family.

Trouble was, she would. Just not on the Welling side.

"We'd better find our seats."

Everyone said goodbyes, and Graham gave Mattie one

last hug. "You're going to do great. I'll be praying for you the whole time."

Mattie nodded, and then Graham walked with his parents into the auditorium. They found Phillip and Belinda at their reserved seats. Everyone greeted each other, then filled in the row. Graham ended up in the aisle seat, his father next to him.

"You never mentioned what Lucy looks like."

He kept his gaze forward, hoping to avoid this conversation.

"Or that you had feelings for her."

A quick glance told him Phillip and Belinda weren't overhearing his father. "I don't, Dad. Or at least I can't."

"Why not?"

"You already know why not. You know what they—" he nodded down the row "—said and did. It will never work. I can't do that to Mattie."

"Do what? Give her a new family? A stepmom?"

The last word echoed in the suddenly silent auditorium as the lights faded. Graham leaned forward enough to check on the Wellings with his peripheral vision. They were conversing with his mom, or rather his mom was talking and they were nodding.

"No. Take someone else away from her. If something happens with Lucy, Mattie will lose having a relationship with her grandparents. We're already barely keeping the turmoil of our current relationship from her."

"I think you're giving them too much power."

"I don't think I have a choice in the matter."

"Of course, you're praying about it and asking for God's guidance. Not trying to figure out everything on your own."

Graham resisted squirming like a little boy in trouble. "Of course." He had prayed about all of it many times. Graham got up at six every morning and read his Bible and prayed. He lifted up his concerns, trusting God to handle everything. But he couldn't help but wonder if somewhere along the way, maybe he'd stopped believing God could work this out.

At least, in the way Graham wanted Him to.

Besides, he already had so much good in his life. Who was he to ask for more?

Chapter Fifteen

Good thing breathing was an autonomic reflex, because Graham had spent the first half of the performance forgetting to fill his lungs with oxygen.

Mattie had already done one dance earlier in the evening, and she'd absolutely beamed from the stage. She'd even missed a step or two and hadn't flinched once. Most of the girls in Mattie's class had forgotten what they were doing for a portion of the dance, stopping to watch the other girls before remembering they were part of it. After seeing that, Graham had finally relaxed. No one was expecting the little girls to be perfect. In fact, their small missteps were endearing.

Now Mattie was back out on stage for her second dance. She looked so happy, and Graham owed it all to Lucy.

His mind flashed back to that day in the parking lot when Lucy had grabbed Mattie's car seat without asking and completely changed their lives. In the past two weeks, Graham had hoped the feelings he'd developed for Lucy would change.

His wish had come true. They had changed. Just not in the way he'd wanted. They'd increased. And he didn't have a clue what to do about it. Today had been Lucy's last day of work at his office—and a half day at that, since she'd needed to prepare for tonight's recital. On Monday, Hollie was returning from maternity leave and Lucy wouldn't be working for him anymore. Graham didn't know her plan. And according to the Wellings, he shouldn't care so much.

But he did.

To say he'd miss her would be the understatement of the century.

Mattie stepped forward from the line of girls and did a few steps on her own.

She looked so mature Graham wanted to cry. If only Brooke could see her. She'd be so proud. She would absolutely love this moment.

Would he ever stop missing her? He imagined not. She'd been his best friend in every way possible. What would she think of these feelings he harbored for Lucy? Would she agree with her parents? Or would she see what he saw?

The dance ended, and the girls ran from the stage, their little shoes pattering. Thundering applause sounded as the next group of older girls took the stage for their dance.

She would have wanted me to be happy.

The thought whispered in his mind, then grabbed hold with intensity. Brooke wouldn't have been okay with the tension circling between him and her parents. But she would have wanted him and Mattie to be happy.

The one thought contradicted the other, leaving Graham completely confused. He didn't know how to handle any of this.

What a mess.

God, show me what I'm missing, what I can't see. Show me Your way. Mine isn't working.

The last group exited the stage, and the owner of the dance school came out. Someone presented her with flowers. After that, all of the dancers filed out on stage. Line after line filled the space. Mattie, being one of the smallest, was in the front.

The audience gave them a standing ovation as they continued to come out. Mattie's class kept getting pushed forward to give the others more room.

When the last group walked out, everyone inched forward another step. Mattie was right on the edge of the stage, but she didn't seem to realize it. When they started to bow, Graham's nerves went on high alert. But Mattie completed the bow and stood back up, pride and delight mingling on her face.

How he loved that little girl.

The audience continued to clap, and the group on stage started a second bow. Only this time, Mattie tipped forward and lost her balance. She wobbled trying to find her footing, and then she toppled right off the stage.

Lucy watched it happen. One moment, Mattie was on stage taking a bow with her class. The next, she was gone, disappearing as if she'd fallen off the side of a cliff. Lucy shoved forward through the dancers until she reached the front. At the sight of a crumpled Mattie, she heard someone scream. She jumped off the stage and bent over the little girl.

Mattie was crying, and somewhere this registered as a relief. She was alive. Granted, the drop was only a few feet, but Lucy's mind had gone wild with fear.

"Talk to me, Mattie Grace. What hurts?"

"My-my-my arrrrrmmmmm." The last word came out as a wail.

Lucy stroked back curls that had jarred loose. "It's okay. You're going to be okay." The words felt like lies, but she continued to whisper them along with a barrage of prayers.

Please let her be okay. Let there be nothing permanent wrong. Please.

Where was Graham? Lucy didn't know what to do. Should she pick Mattie up? She'd heard too many stories of injuries that shouldn't have been moved, and she didn't want to do anything to make it worse. It was her fault that Mattie was here in the first place.

And then Graham was there, kneeling over the other side of Mattie, asking doctor questions instead of father questions, calm and strong. Graham's hands checked over Mattie, and her subsequent cry when he reached her arm made Lucy's stomach lurch.

Graham's parents were right behind him, along with the Wellings. As usual, the couple didn't acknowledge her, but this time Lucy didn't care. She scooted out of the way so that Mattie's family could surround her.

An ambulance arrived, and Lucy backed farther away as they rolled a stretcher in. Mattie would hate all of this attention. Good thing she wasn't coherent enough to realize a crowd stood around her. Lucy would give anything to be able to protect the girl from all of this and from the pain she must be enduring.

Now Lucy finally understood why Graham acted the way he did about Mattie. After this, she'd apologize for ever doubting him. Maybe they could get Mattie one of those protective bubbles.

The crowd parted as the paramedics, Graham and Mattie's grandparents exited the building. Lucy spotted something red on the floor.

Mattie's glasses.

She picked them up. *God, I know she's not mine, but it feels like she is. Please let her be okay. Let her be okay and I'll leave the two of them alone. I'll back away.*

Lucy didn't know where the thought came from. She only knew she wanted Graham and Mattie to be happy. And while the thought that she wasn't the answer to that equation just about killed her, she knew without a doubt that if walking away was what she needed to do…

She wouldn't hesitate.

* * *

Pain medicine was an amazing thing. Mattie had been in the emergency room close to two hours, and she'd gone from wailing in pain to whimpering, and more recently, to being completely distracted by the dilemma of which color cast she wanted for the hairline fracture in her forearm.

Pink.

She didn't need surgery, and because the swelling was minimal, they could get it cast in the ER. While the fall had been a shock, she was fine other than an additional bump on her head. Graham could breathe. Sort of.

"Daddy, do you want to sign my cast first?"

"Sure."

"And then Grandma."

"I'd be honored, love bug." Graham's mom was the one who had stayed with him. At first, both sets of grandparents had been there, but it had been too many people. After everyone learned Mattie was okay, she'd been covered in kisses and then his dad and the Wellings had left.

"I still get to have my sleepover, right?"

Graham exchanged a wide-eyed look with his mom. He brushed some of the loose curls from Mattie's forehead. "Honey, I don't think that's the best idea."

Tears welled. "But Grandma and I were going to celebrate my first dance recital. And she has miniature teacups and marshmallows." Even if Graham did have those things, they wouldn't compare to what his mom had. She was the best at planning special activities with Mattie.

"Maybe we could reschedule?" His mom held Mattie's cup so she could take a sip of water from the straw. "What if we did it next weekend instead?"

Mattie's head swung back and forth, eyes piercing him. "Daddy, you said I could."

"That was before you hurt your arm. Don't you want to sleep in your own bed?" He couldn't imagine being away from her tonight. She might not need him, but he needed her. He wanted to check on her fifty times and see her tousled hair on her pillow.

She contemplated that question. "I do kind of want to see my stuffies. They need to know what happened to me."

He resisted a smile.

"What if I drive you home?" His mom glanced at him, and he nodded. "And we get to have a cup of hot chocolate before bed. I'll tuck you in, but you'll still get to be in your own bed..." She smiled. "Where your father can watch you like a hawk."

"Mom."

She laughed. "What? You are overprotective. In the best way, of course." Her hand patted his cheek. "Between you and your sisters, we endured all kinds of nights of worry. And just look how great you turned out. I always had a feeling—"

"No feelings, Mom. I can't handle hearing about one tonight."

"Just let me say something about Lucy."

He shot his mother a look that said she should know better with Mattie in the room. "Nope. Not happening. None of your feelings are allowed. I should have made that a requirement for you being the one who got to stay."

She huffed, a line splitting her brow. "Fine. But don't say I didn't warn you."

"Warn me about what?" Graham waved a hand. "Never mind. I don't want to know."

"Where is Lucy?" Mattie piped up. "How come I haven't seen her? Why isn't she here?"

"I'm sure she had to finish up recital stuff."

"Oh." Her nose wrinkled. "Okay. But I want to see her soon."

He saluted Mattie. "Yes, ma'am."

She laughed, gluing back together the pieces of his heart that had shattered when she'd fallen off the stage. But the smug look his mother wore wasn't giving him any peace. He should have had his dad stay.

Thankfully, Dr. Kent chose that moment to reappear. "The good news is we have pink. The bad news is I got caught with another patient. Sorry about that."

"No problem. We don't mind waiting." When they'd left the recital, Graham hadn't known the exact nature of Mattie's injury or if it would require surgery. The fact that they'd arrived at the ER to find Dr. Kent—the best orthopedic specialist Graham knew—already on call because of another patient had practically brought Graham to his knees with gratefulness.

An hour later, Mattie's arm was cast and they were ready to head out the door. Pretty impressive by ER standards. No doubt they were getting the royal treatment.

He picked up an exhausted Mattie from the bed and she wrapped around him. He kissed the top of her hair as he walked, feet grinding to a halt when he caught sight of Lucy in the waiting room.

She was curled into a horribly uncomfortable-looking chair, head tipped to her shoulder, sleeping. If his heart could jump from his chest, it would have.

His mom pried Mattie from his arms. "Go." She nodded toward Lucy. "I'm driving Mattie home, remember? Don't mess this up. Not everyone gets a second chance at love."

"It's not like that." His words fell on an empty waiting room as his mom and Mattie disappeared. Graham walked slowly to Lucy, his pulse erratic.

He sat in the chair next to her and allowed himself to slide a hand along her cheek. "Lucy, honey. Wake up."

Her eyelids fluttered open, lips curving in a soft smile. "Hi." Those same eyes widened. "How's Mattie? I was waiting for so long, I just thought I'd rest for a minute and then—"

"She's fine. Just a hairline fracture."

A crease cut through Lucy's forehead. "Just? Just? If I

hadn't forced her into dance class, none of this would have happened. You warned me. You said she always got injured in sports, but I told you to let go. I—"

"You were right. I did need to let go."

Her head shook quickly. "No. Not true. We need to get her a bubble or something. I can't handle her being hurt, Graham. I get it."

His lips slid up. "We're not getting her a bubble." *We*. He liked the sound of that. As if they were a team. "Though it's not a bad idea."

Tears slid down Lucy's cheeks. "Why do my eyes keep doing this?" She swiped away moisture. "I'm not a crier, but my eyes keep leaking. It's annoying."

He reached to the side table and snagged a tissue for her. "After all of my worrying, she did get injured, but you know what? She was still full of excitement about her first recital once her pain medicine kicked in. She wouldn't have traded tonight for anything. She was even telling me about how she could dance with a broken arm and how she was glad it wasn't a foot. If I'd kept her from doing it, she wouldn't have learned all she did these last few weeks. She's really come out of her shell."

Lucy sniffled. "She has. But I'm still so sorry. I wasn't even going to come here, but I just had to know if she was okay. Guess I'd better follow through on my promise."

"What promise?"

"Nothing." Lucy grabbed her purse and stood, her body swaying.

He jumped up and put an arm around her. "I don't think you should be driving, Duchess. You look a bit out of it."

"I'm fine." Her eyelids slid shut and she leaned against him. "It's annoying you always smell so good."

His mouth hitched. "I apologize." He didn't know what had got into her, but Lucy was acting all sorts of strange.

"I didn't sleep well last night. I was thinking about the performance and going over things in my head."

She shuffled her feet, and Graham tightened his hold around her as they walked out the doors.

"I don't function well with a lack of sleep."

"I'm gathering that."

Her arm tucked around his back. "Did I mention you smell good?"

"Once or twice."

She moaned. "It's like I don't have a filter right now."

"Then I should come up with all kinds of questions to ask you." Graham got to his car and opened the passenger door, almost getting Lucy inside before she balked.

"Wait. What are you doing?"

"Driving you home."

"Absolutely not." She backed away from the vehicle. "I have my car here."

"We'll get it tomorrow." He nudged her into the seat. Amazingly she went, though she grumbled the whole way.

He walked around to the driver's side and got in.

She dug through her purse. "Here." She handed him Mattie's glasses.

"Thanks." He put them in the console. "I wondered what happened to those."

"And I can't see you tomorrow."

"Okay." He started the car and drove out of the lot. "Why not?"

"I'm not going to see you or Mattie. I told God if He would help Mattie not to be seriously injured, I'd get out of your lives."

Panic kicked in. "That's not how God works, Lucy, and you know it."

She crossed her arms. Stared out the window. "I know," she whispered, voice burdened with sadness. "But I just needed to feel like I was doing something to make her better. I just need to feel...useful. I don't like waiting for things to get better on their own."

"I know. You're my fix-it girl. But you can't stay away

from me and Mattie. We need you… I mean, she needs you." The correction was a lie. He did need Lucy. But what could he do about it? Talk to the Wellings? They didn't show any signs of changing their minds. Tonight, even with how proud they'd been of Mattie and knowing Lucy had been the one to get her into dance, they hadn't mentioned her once. Not one thank-you. Not even an acknowledgment of all she'd done for their granddaughter.

He felt helpless. As though he had two paths before him and he wanted them both. How was he supposed to choose between Lucy and Mattie's grandparents? It was impossible. He needed to drop Lucy off as fast as possible and then run from her. Literally. Even if he had to get out of the car and sprint. Because resisting her was not something he could accomplish right now.

After a few instructions, Graham pulled into the driveway for Lucy's apartment, past the small red house near the street. He parked beside the garage, then shifted toward her.

She wouldn't look at him.

He slid a hand under her chin, gently turning her face to him. "Lucy, you're the best thing that's happened to Mattie in years. Stop beating yourself up about this."

"I'm trying." She mirrored his position, her shoulder against the seat, her face mere inches from his.

He wanted nothing more than to kiss her. But how could he do that when he knew it couldn't go anywhere? It would be torture to feel her lips on his and never have that experience again. It had been hard enough the last time, and that lip-lock had barely registered on the kissing scale.

Graham grasped for something to veto the thoughts running through his head. The other week, Lucy had mentioned a date. Was she still dating someone? Though the thought shattered him, it would give him the strength he needed to step back from her.

"Lucy, are you dating someone?"

Relief and frustration warred at the thought. *Please say*

yes. Make it easier for me to walk away from you. Although, really, would anything make that easier for him to do?

Her head swung from side to side. "Not anymore. You kind of ruined that for me."

"I'm sorry."

Her eyebrow quirked. "Really?"

A wry laugh slipped out. "Not really."

When her lips curved, he couldn't tear his eyes from them. From her. "Lucy." His voice was hoarse, pleading. "I need you to get out of the car."

She didn't move.

"Duchess, for once in your life…" He tried to infuse humor into his tone, but it just came out threaded with desperation. "Will you please listen to me?"

He was asking her to walk away, but how could she?

Graham studied her with serious eyes, and Lucy could see the truth in their evergreen depths. Something—someone— still held him back. Was it Brooke? The Wellings? She only knew whatever it was would break her heart. But even still, she couldn't force herself to run for safety.

Which meant Lucy would be crushed. She should listen to Graham and get out of this car right now. She should yell about the unfairness of it all. Or cry. Definitely cry. But more than she wanted to protect herself, she wanted him.

In this moment, even if she only had this moment, she just wanted to believe they had a chance, that his in-laws or Brooke didn't stand between them.

That she was enough.

She slid one hand across his cheek, fingertips meeting smooth, close-shaved skin. He stayed still, watching her, his breathing as shallow as a Colorado creek bed during a drought. She inched forward. Touched her lips to his. Waited while indecision warred on his face.

And then her name was a groan, and he was kissing

her with such tenderness that new tears sprang behind her closed eyelids.

His arms went around her, and she sank into the essence of Graham. The way he smelled, the taste of him. Her fingers roamed behind his neck, sliding into his hair.

She could drown in his kiss and not regret it.

Until tomorrow. Tomorrow, the memory would haunt her.

But tonight…tonight she planned to live in this moment.

Chapter Sixteen

"Wait a minute." Olivia ate a spoonful of her ice cream sundae and propped her feet on Lucy's coffee table. "So if you didn't see Graham this morning after all of that, how'd you get your car back?"

"I jogged to get it."

Liv's head swung from watching the chick flick they'd seen too many times to count to Lucy's spot at the other end of the couch.

She looked up from her bowl of ice cream and met her sister's gaze. "What? It was only a few miles."

"And Graham was okay with that?" Olivia tapped her spoon against her bowl, brow wrinkled. "Maybe I need to change my opinion of the man."

"It had nothing to do with Graham. I needed my car. I got my car. I texted him I didn't need a ride. He probably thought I was getting one from you."

Olivia rolled her eyes. "Good to know that these changes I've been seeing in you aren't all-encompassing."

Lucy laughed.

"So, did you discuss anything after the kiss?"

Lucy set her bowl on the coffee table, digestion suddenly vetoing the idea of more ice cream. "Just that it wouldn't be happening again." Information that hadn't come as a surprise but still hurt. Graham had told her nothing could come of their kiss.

The man had kissed her until she couldn't breathe or think straight, then tried to apologize.

She'd wanted to cry and slap him and kiss him all over again. An unusual combination. But she'd settled on accepting. Why? Because she'd known going into that kiss it wouldn't lead anywhere.

"What?" Olivia shrieked. "You can't just leave it like that."

"Actually, we can."

Flashing blue eyes that were an exact match for Lucy's bored into her with impressive heat.

"It's…complicated."

"Did you at least tell him you love him?"

Good thing she'd stopped eating or Lucy would have choked. "I don't—" Lucy sat back against the couch cushions. "I can't love him."

Liv's eyebrows scrunched together. "Why not?"

"I'm not…enough. There's something holding him back. And I'm certain part of it, if not all, is his in-laws. We don't stand a chance at a relationship with them between us. And…" Lucy trailed off.

"And what?"

"I'm not sure I am right for Graham and Mattie. I want them, but…what if the Wellings' obvious misgivings about me are right? I'm young and not exactly mature. Could a relationship with Graham and me even work? I mean, it's not like I'm mom material."

Olivia let out a disgusted snort. "Says who?" She looked ready to pop up from the couch and hunt down the person who dared to offend her little sister. Bless her.

"Probably everyone. Again, including his in-laws."

"What did I tell you about that?" With a growl, Olivia set her bowl on the coffee table. It landed with a clatter. "It doesn't matter what his in-laws think. It matters what God thinks. The Wellings are wrong, Lulu."

Lucy had her doubts. "Even if that's true, what can I do about it?"

Silence reigned. The fact that Liv looked at a loss for answers didn't encourage Lucy in the least.

"I thought you knew everything, big sister."

"I don't. But I have learned to pray before doing." She grinned. "Most of the time."

Lucy thought she had, too. But it turned out she really, really stank at asking God for help. She still struggled against the tendency to do everything on her own. And whenever she did get into the habit of praying and asking first, she always ended up snatching things back and attempting to do them herself again. Just like after the recital, thinking she could fix everything by not seeing Graham or Mattie. Why couldn't she just hand things over and trust God? Why did she think she could handle everything on her own? If the past few weeks were any indication, she definitely could not.

"I still think you love him."

"Like you so willingly admitted you loved Cash? I remember visiting, sister. I think everyone knew you loved him before you did."

Instead of taking offense, Liv just laughed. "Probably true. Nice try changing the subject."

"I don't—" Lucy huffed, ready to deny that she loved Graham, but the words caught in her throat. She hadn't... She couldn't...

No.

The realization washed over her with a certainty she couldn't ignore. Oh, stink. How had she let that happen? She'd known not to let her feelings for Graham progress, but they'd just gone on and done their own thing, tumbling all the way to heartbreak land.

Her eyes closed. "Fine. I love him." Guess all of that

wanting him to be happy even if it wasn't with her did stem from her growing love for Graham and Mattie. Fluttering started in her stomach. "I love him."

A smile formed, then dropped like a stone. "But I still can't have him." She turned to Liv. "Will you *please* stop making me feel things? You're the worst sister ever."

"And by that you mean the best?" Olivia beamed, and they both laughed, though Lucy's ended on a pathetic note. She might love Graham, but she didn't have a clue what to do about it.

As the movie progressed, Lucy's mind wouldn't settle. One tempting but nerve-racking idea kept taking hold. There was something she could do with her recently discovered feelings. She could tell Graham. Give him the words as a gift. He might not be able or willing to say them back to her...but wasn't the point of love to give it away?

Never had a text sent him into cardiac arrest before, but Graham was pretty sure the one he'd received from Lucy ten minutes ago on his way out of church had done exactly that.

I need you.

Lucy Grayson—the girl who had turned his life upside down, the one he'd kissed two nights ago and hadn't stopped thinking about since—never needed anyone.

The text had included an address, so he'd replied that he and Mattie would head in her direction. Graham had asked what was wrong, but he'd yet to receive an answer from Lucy. Surely his elevated blood pressure would come down once he found out she was okay.

Graham spotted Lucy's car and parked two spots over. "Mattie, I'll be right outside the car. Just stay buckled in."

"But I want to see Lucy."

"You will. Just give me a sec."

He popped out, striding in her direction.

Was she having car trouble? Another flat tire? What in the world had happened?

She was standing by the passenger door of her car. Smiling. Heart attack number two of his day.

"What's wrong?" He stopped in front of her, grabbing her hands. They were freezing, and it wasn't cold out. "Lucy, what's going on? I'm going nuts here."

Her smile was like sunshine. He shouldn't look at it, but he couldn't tear away.

"How's Mattie?" She waved at the backseat of his car, and Mattie grinned, waving back with her non-cast arm.

"Really?" Exasperation laced his tone. "That's how we're going to play a desperate text and me finding you on the side of the road?"

"You didn't find me. I asked you to come. And I'm in a parking spot, not on the side of the road." Again, her lips curved as though she harbored a tantalizing secret. "And, yes, that's what I want to know."

He knew better than to fight this woman. "Mattie's great. She did way better than I expected the last two nights. We even made it to church this morning."

"I know." Her head tilted. "I saw you across the way, but the two of you were surrounded by a crowd."

A rush of pride gripped him. "It's a bit surprising, but I think she might be learning to enjoy the attention." Mattie was changing, opening up, and most if not all of the credit for that went to the woman currently standing in front of him. The one confusing him with her cryptic texts and giddy behavior.

"Smart girl."

"So, any chance you're going to tell me what's going on now?"

Whatever it was, Lucy certainly found it amusing. "I guess." She released a mock sigh. "You know how you walk over those grate things in the ground and think, man, it sure would be awful to drop your keys in there?"

"No." This woman was crazy. "I've never thought that."

"Yes, you have! Everyone has thought that."

"Lucy." At her name grinding between his teeth, she pointed to the ground.

"I actually did that. I stopped after church to grab a sandwich and a Diet Coke, and then *bam*, down they went."

He glanced to where she was pointing, then bent to peer closer. Sure enough, a pink ballet-slipper keychain was wedged a few feet down in a pile of muck. A bit of trash. Some food.

When he straightened, she was beaming again. Was she going to start bouncing on her toes next? "Did you drop them on purpose?"

"No." Her eyes widened with innocence. "It was an accident."

"Then why are you so happy about it?"

"At first, I was just upset. I was trying to decide whether to walk home—if I had an extra set of keys there—"

"Why would you do that? Of course you should call—"

"Wait!" She held up a hand. "And then I realized something." The look on her face softened from humor to something entirely different. She edged slightly closer, bringing with her the smell of lime and coconut. "I realized I *wanted* to ask you to help me. I wanted to be rescued. By you."

His hand lifted involuntarily, tucking a loose curl behind her ear. "You asked for help? And you wanted to?"

She nodded.

Who knew what a heady feeling that thought could invoke? His mouth hovered way too close to hers. "I should get Mattie out of the car. She wants to see you. Plus, I have no doubt if I don't, in the next few seconds, I'm going to be kissing you." The past two nights, he'd barely slept between checking on Mattie and thinking about that kiss from Friday night. *Kisses.*

Goose bumps erupted on Lucy's arms, and Graham rubbed his hands across her bare skin. She was wearing a sundress, gray on top, colorful zigzag stripes on the bottom. As always, she looked gorgeous.

Graham had spent the past day and a half thinking about her, processing whether a relationship between them might be possible.

Was there a chance for them? The weight of that question rested on his shoulders. He couldn't tell Lucy how he felt about her until he'd dealt with the Wellings. And he wasn't exactly sure how to do that. Another thought that had kept him awake.

"Kissing." Her head swung back and forth and those lips smoothed together. "Can't have that."

"Unfortunately not." Or maybe just *not yet*.

Somehow, he managed to drag himself away from her, go to his car and open the back door for Mattie. She scrambled out, shooting him a look that said the minute he'd left her in there had been far too long.

She vaulted into Lucy's arms. "Are you coming to lunch with us? Daddy said I get to have a celebration lunch and I want you to come."

Lucy had crouched for a hug, and now she met his gaze over the top of Mattie's head. "I'm not so sure—"

"We should celebrate two things. Mattie's dance recital and your recent…groundbreaking decision."

Her eyes crinkled. After another Mattie squeeze, she stood, her hand still wrapped around his daughter's. A seriousness rare for Lucy tugged at her features. "Are you sure that's a good idea? I know there's things—"

"It's just lunch." That wasn't true, and they both knew it. They had things to discuss, to figure out, but he just wanted to spend a little time with her. Hollie would be back from maternity leave tomorrow, and Graham likely wouldn't see much of Lucy this week. The thought was enough to make him consider begging.

She nodded. "Okay. It's just lunch."

They loaded into his car. "We'll have to get a hanger or something to get the keys out. So, food or keys first?"

Mattie and Lucy exchanged a grin, both answering "Food" at the same time.

"Let's go to our place, Daddy."

"Which one's our place?"

"The one we went to with Lucy before. The one with ice cream."

Our place. Lucy smiled, and Graham wanted to lean over and kiss the spot where it creased her cheek. The idea of it being *their* place swept in and took hold. Graham was done trying to stay away from Lucy. If rescuing her from lost keys made him this happy, he couldn't fight how he felt any longer.

He needed to talk to Phillip and Belinda.

After the short drive there, the three of them piled out of the car. Mattie held Lucy's hand, and Graham barely resisted doing the same.

He wanted this—the three of them together. He just wasn't sure how to get it. Would the Wellings even listen to him?

His gut churned at the thought. Graham needed to orchestrate things right, because he didn't want to lose anyone from Mattie's life. Somehow he had to figure out how to get through to the couple.

They were almost to the register when Mattie started hopping on one foot. "Dad, I have to go potty."

"I'll take her," Lucy said. "Order me that sandwich again." And before he could protest, they were gone.

He shouldn't have been surprised when Phillip and Belinda opened the door of the restaurant and stepped inside. Graham knew they ate out every Sunday after church, and—how could he forget?—he'd even run into them here before. Still, when Mattie had suggested it, the Wellings showing up had never crossed his mind.

Of course, he'd been preoccupied with thoughts of Lucy. She had that effect on him.

At first, the sight of them sent him into a small panic. They would be irate about him being here with Lucy after their previous conversation. But then…that fear turned into something else.

Excitement.

He wanted to talk to them. Why not now? Waiting wasn't going to get him any closer to having Lucy in his life. Graham was done tiptoeing around them. They had to be able to talk calmly and work this out.

He left his place in line and strode over to them. "Phillip, Belinda." He greeted them with stiff hugs. "Could I speak to you outside for a minute?"

They nodded, looks instantly changing to concern. Once outside, Graham fumbled for words. Perhaps he should have given himself some time to figure out what he wanted to say and how to say it.

"Where's Mattie?"

He hadn't thought about that question being asked so quickly, though it made perfect sense. "She's…using the restroom."

"Oh." Belinda nodded. "And is her arm okay? How's she feeling?"

"She's doing well. We went to late church. She wanted to go, I think to show off her cast." His mouth quirked at that, but he quickly came back to what he wanted to talk to them about. "But Mattie's not in the restroom by herself."

Now their faces twisted with confusion. And really—he resisted an eye roll—he could have come up with a better intro than that.

"She's with Lucy."

Phillip glanced to his wife, then Graham. "Isn't Lucy done working for you?"

What did that have to do with anything? "Friday was her last day. Hollie comes back on Monday."

"Then why is Lucy here with you? You're not holding up your end of the deal. You said after Lucy stopped working for you, she'd be out of your life."

Graham choked on his breath. Scrubbed a hand over the back of his neck. "I never said that. You assumed. That was never part of our deal."

"Grandpa, Grandma!" Mattie's squeal echoed down Main Street. She flew by Graham in a blur, lurching into her grandfather's arms. He chuckled and began asking Mattie questions about her arm as Lucy stopped next to Graham, confusion marring her brow.

"What did you just say about a deal? What's going on?"

Panic filled his mouth with a metallic taste. This wasn't going according to plan. Not that he'd had a great one of those when he'd stepped outside in the first place.

Graham needed to talk to Lucy. Alone.

He tried to steady his voice, though it didn't obey. "Phillip, Belinda. Can you take Mattie inside and order?"

The couple stared, their wounded looks flashing between him and Lucy.

"I'll be right there. Please."

After what felt like an hour, they acquiesced. Graham waited for the restaurant door to shut before facing Lucy.

He reached for her hand. Held on. "Remember when the Wellings were upset the night they came over and you were there?"

She nodded.

"They were concerned about me dating."

"You said that."

A sigh rumbled through his chest. "But I didn't tell you the rest of it. They said if I dated you, they'd walk out of Mattie's life. And I couldn't do that to her. I couldn't let her lose another person. And so I promised not to date you."

She pulled her hand away from his as though his touch scalded. "You...you made a deal over me?"

"It wasn't like that."

A wounded sound tore from her throat. "Did you or did you not make an agreement with them about me and then not tell me about it?" Though quiet and controlled, her words pierced like a knife.

He wanted to lie so badly. He needed time to explain. Needed her to stop looking at him with so much hurt bursting from her blue eyes. "Yes, but you have to understand—"

"I understand." Her wooden response slayed him. Tears glistened, but she blinked them away, replacing them with a vacant look that scared him even more. "I knew I wasn't good enough for them. But I had no idea you felt the same way."

"That's not true." Graham's world was spinning out of control. "You know I don't think that way about you."

"If you were willing to use me as a bargaining chip, then yes, you do." Fingertips pressed against her lips. "And I had to go and fall in love with you."

What? His throat constricted, but she didn't give him any time to deal with that comment.

"I'd wanted to tell you, wanted you to know how much I felt for you even though I knew you couldn't say it back to me." Her eyelids momentarily shuttered. "Now I know why."

His fingers itched to reach for her, to hold her there. Knowing she wouldn't tolerate his touch, Graham fisted his hands by his sides.

"I was going to tell you that you should move on without me. I wanted you to be happy. To find someone they approved of." She motioned toward the restaurant. "I'd hoped you wouldn't go back to the place you were in before, that you'd get married and have more kids." Her head shook as though she could wish away the pain written on her face. "I knew better. I knew better than to fall in love."

She took a step back.

He panicked. "Lucy, please listen to me. I didn't know what else to do. They didn't give me any choice. I couldn't—"

"Goodbye, Graham." She turned and walked away. With each step, a piece of him crumbled.

"Wait!" he called out. "Your keys. We need to get them out. At least let me drive you—"

She whirled in his direction, what felt like miles of sidewalk separating them. "Don't worry, noble Graham. I'll take care of it myself." Her shoulders straightened, mouth weighed down with sadness that resonated in his bones. "I always do." She sounded hollow. No tears. No yelling at him.

He wanted to go after her, to make her listen. He wanted to be the person she called when she needed help. But he'd ruined any chance of rescuing Lucy. *For the rest of my life?*

Had he lost her forever? That goodbye had been full of finality. Graham shook off the thought because it was drowning him, snaking around his chest and squeezing until he couldn't breathe.

He got out his cell and texted Cash.

Your SIL is walking down Main near Adams. Needs help getting keys out of a drain.

The next bit was harder to type.

Won't let me help her.

She would have, five minutes ago. Before Graham had thrown away any hope of a future between them. He couldn't believe he'd failed her.

And the fact that she loved him…had loved him, at least. What was the point of doing life without Lucy?

Mattie.

He dug his fingers into his temples, but nothing quieted the humming pain that had taken over his body.

Mattie would be distraught. She loved Lucy fiercely.

He'd done all of this to prevent Mattie from losing another person, yet now that was exactly what had happened.

He wasn't the only one suffering in this scenario.

His phone buzzed with a reply text.

Got it. Liv's on the way. Trouble between you 2?

A wry breath puffed out of him.

Something like that.

Cash's reply came quickly.

Been there, done that. Hang in there. Grayson girls usually come around.

Graham wanted to believe his friend so badly, but hope felt too far out of reach.

That was that. Olivia would help Lucy. Graham was no longer a necessary part of her life. He had been for about two minutes. And maybe it would have lasted if he'd handled things better or stood up to his in-laws earlier.

He should never have let things escalate the way they had. Though he still didn't have answers, he only knew he'd failed to figure it out before it was too late.

A failure. He knew the feeling well. He let it wrap around him, accepting the blame he deserved.

All of those things Lucy had said about him moving on and not going back…getting married. Having more kids.

What she didn't know—what she would never know now—was that this time he didn't need a few hours to process. He already agreed with her. He *was* meant to do all of those things. He was just meant to do them with her.

Chapter Seventeen

Olivia paused in the doorway to Lucy's bedroom. "Any chance you've stopped wallowing between the time I walked out of your room five minutes ago and my return?"

Considering that it was Saturday evening and Lucy was still lounging in bed dressed in orange striped pajama pants and a white long-sleeved T-shirt, the answer to Olivia's question should most likely be no.

"I'm not wallowing. A girl should be able to stay in her pajamas all day if she wants to. It's not a crime. And who even uses that word anyway? Wallow. It sounds funny. Like something a fish would do."

Her sister dropped onto the other side of the bed, facing her. "Fish don't wallow. They swim."

"Enough with that word! I hereby ban all words that start with *W* for the rest of the night."

"Oh, Lulu." An amused sigh slipped from Olivia. "You're definitely snarky enough to drive any man away."

"Hey! I didn't drive him away. He made a deal over me." A new ache started in Lucy's chest, right next to the wound that had been ripped open last Sunday. "Like I was a chess piece," she whispered. "Or a business merger."

"Yeah. I'm not a big fan of that, either. But don't you know him better than that? Don't you think he had reasons?

I agree he shouldn't have done that, but he was just trying to protect Mattie—"

"I get that part of it." Lucy would do anything for Mattie, too, so she understood Graham had been put in a hard place. "But how could he not tell me? How could he have an agreement with them about me and not say a thing? How could he trade me like that? I just feel…"

Used. Worthless. Lucy swallowed the words. "I knew I wasn't good enough for the Wellings, and that was hard enough. But Graham?" Those annoying tears she'd been fighting all week tried to return, but she blinked them away.

Enough of this. So she'd been hurt. She needed to pull herself back together. And she certainly wasn't going to admit she was doing the *W* word her sister had mentioned.

How could Lucy miss something so much that she'd never had? It had been six days since that awful moment with Graham and his in-laws, and she hadn't seen or heard from him since. And since she no longer worked at his office…not a glimpse of him all week.

Six days somehow equaled a year in her math world.

She was mad at him and she missed him all at the same time. She wanted to yell at him. She wanted him to show up on her doorstep and kiss her, to hear him say he'd fixed everything with his in-laws and he was a jerk of the biggest sort.

But even if he did all of those things…she still couldn't let go of how she'd felt in that moment. He'd made her feel like the yucky stuff that had been sticking to her keys when she'd finally retrieved them from under the grate.

How could she just forget that?

It would be like forgetting about Mattie, and Lucy knew after this week that was something she could never do.

The spring dance session had ended after last week's recital, so she hadn't seen Mattie since the confrontation with Graham. Lucy missed the girl and was desperate to know if she was okay.

Was Mattie and Graham's relationship with the Wellings intact? And why did Lucy care so much? The couple had been nothing but horrible to her, but still, she didn't want anything to stand between them and their granddaughter.

Maybe tonight, after Olivia left, Lucy would go over to Graham's to check on Mattie. Make sure things were okay between her and the Wellings. And if they weren't? Lucy would march over there and set the couple straight. Forget hiding out. Nobody put Lucy in a corner. It was time to hit the dance floor again. Just minus the partner she'd hoped to have.

Except…before Lucy stormed over there attempting to fix everything herself, she would pray about it. It still might not be her first instinct to stop and ask God for help, but she planned to train herself the way a person would train a puppy.

Olivia would probably start studying numerous devotionals, verses and books, but Lucy had trouble with all that. One word seemed possible for her. So one word was what she'd chosen. It was the one that had been knocking her over the head for the past few weeks, and she'd finally recognized God's direction.

Ask.

And so she was working on it. It had been a long time coming, this change in her. But she'd finally hit bottom. Finally realized she couldn't do everything on her own. A simple paper sat on her nightstand, the word *Ask* scrawled in her handwriting. Her reminder to do exactly that. And each morning for the past week, Lucy had paused before doing anything else in her day and asked God for help.

Her prayers weren't eloquent. They were more the accumulation of many years of thinking she could handle it all herself. And the new realization that she couldn't.

Some days, she didn't even know what she was asking for.

Maybe God preferred it that way, without all of her suggestions and solutions added in.

"You've had a week to process," Olivia said, breaking into her thoughts. "What are you going to do now? You can't keep living like this. Don't you think you need to forgive Graham even if you two aren't together?"

Lucy scooted farther under her covers. "I didn't bug you when you were a mess over Cash."

"True. But Janie did. She was all over me about it."

"Even if I do forgive him, that doesn't change anything between me and the Wellings." She sighed, though it came out as more of a wheeze. "I feel strange." She rubbed a hand over her throat. "Kind of itchy or something." Of course, with the amount of weird things they'd eaten tonight—total junk-food nation—she could very easily feel sick.

Or it could be the fact that she'd lost the man and the little girl she loved. For a second, at the restaurant, she'd let herself believe.

Believe she and Graham had a chance of making things work.

Believe she could be mom material.

Why had she got so involved? When she'd moved here, she'd had a plan, and it hadn't looked like this. There was a reason she didn't do serious. Because it stinking hurt.

The first time she'd met the Wellings, Lucy should have started distancing herself from Mattie and Graham.

"Lucy." Olivia leaned forward. "I think you're breaking out in hives. Are you allergic to something we ate tonight?"

"How should I know? We ate a bunch of junk and then topped it off with dessert. Who knows what was in all of it?"

Her sister's brow creased. "I think you need to go to the hospital."

"What? I'm fine."

"You're not fine. Does your throat feel tight, like you can't get air through?"

"Maybe." Panic began to beat in her veins. "Yes."

Olivia was already running from the room. "I'm grabbing you some Benadryl in case it helps. Let's go!"

Lucy should call Graham. He'd know what to do. But, then again, did he even care? It wasn't as if she'd heard from him this week. She didn't need him or his help. She pushed off the covers and popped out of bed, causing the paper from her nightstand to flutter to the floor.

Ask.

The blatant reminder was just what she needed. Lucy might not have Graham, but she did have God. And He could handle every request she sent His way.

Including her strange combination of symptoms: hives, a swollen throat and a broken heart.

"So, you've been bright and full of sunshine this week." Graham's father handed him a dish he'd just washed, and Graham dried. "Reminds me of that stage you went through in high school when you turned caveman and stopped talking to us for a year. Then one morning your door opened and you were back. It was the strangest thing."

The serving dish clanked as Graham stacked it in the cupboard. Maybe he could just pretend not to hear his dad talking.

"Have you decided what you're going to do?"

Then again, maybe not. "No." Frustration seeped out in a deep sigh. "What can I do? Lucy's mad at me and I deserve it. I was a jerk to have an agreement with the Wellings and not tell her what was going on. Phillip and Belinda are upset and barely speaking to me, though thankfully they are still talking to Mattie. How can I choose? Not that Lucy would even have me at this point. My hands are tied. If I fight for Lucy, Mattie misses out on a relationship with the Wellings. If I choose the Wellings, Mattie and I both miss out on a relationship with Lucy."

There were a lot of bad things about this situation, but

the worst part was that both of his girls were hurting and Graham couldn't fix it. That he'd caused it.

Ever since losing Brooke he'd felt a sense of failure. Could he have done more? What had he missed? Now it all came rushing back. He wanted to fix this. He wanted Lucy *and* Mattie *and* the Wellings to be happy, but after a week of thinking, praying and begging God for guidance, he still didn't know what to do.

"I can't fathom losing a child like the Wellings did, and an only child at that. They must be hurting so much."

"I know. That's why I can't hurt them more."

The water sloshed in the sink, joining the sound of Graham's mom reading to Mattie in the living room. Being at his parents' house always felt comfortable, but tonight it only reminded Graham of what he'd begun to hope he'd have with Lucy.

A home. A family. A person. He just wanted another person meant for him. Was that so much to ask? According to the Wellings, and now Lucy, yes.

"Have you tried talking to them calmly? Outside of them finding you with Lucy?" His dad handed him a bowl.

Graham contemplated that question, a bit surprised by the answer. "No. I guess not."

"Maybe you should try it."

"Dad, they've been so…not themselves. So harsh about Lucy. I don't think that conversation would end well."

Another minute went by in silence.

"Of course, you'll never know unless you try. Plus, I think part of their issue is that you never told them how you feel about Lucy. They just kept finding you with her after you said you weren't dating her."

Exactly what Graham had hoped to talk to them about at the bakery before his life had crashed and burned for the second time. And now all he could think about was how Lucy would love that he'd just inadvertently thought a phrase from *Top Gun*.

"This conversation proves I share way too much with you."

His dad chuckled.

But the man was right. Graham hadn't been honest with the Wellings. Not once had he sat down with Belinda and Phillip and been truthful about his feelings for Lucy—partly because he'd been too busy denying how he really felt.

All of this time, he'd blamed the Wellings for keeping them apart. And while they obviously had reservations about him moving on, Graham believed they were more wounded about missing their daughter than anything else. Each time they'd found him with Lucy—just like last week—it had come as a shock to them.

Things might be different if he'd changed his response to them. He could have said *I think I do have feelings for Lucy, but no matter what happens, you'll always be in Mattie's life.*

He could have reassured them instead of getting defensive.

Graham's phone buzzed in his pocket and he checked the screen. It was the after-hours answering service for the clinic.

He answered.

"Dr. Redmond, Bill Fitzer's son called and said his dad just went back into the hospital. They were hoping you could check on him. He knows he's not technically your patient, but—"

"I'll go. Thanks for letting me know." After a few more details, they disconnected.

Dad dried his hands on the towel. "I heard. Go on. We'll keep Mattie." He paused. "You're a good doctor, you know that?"

Where had that come from? "You're my dad. You have to say that."

"You care, Graham. That's most of the battle right there.

Not every doctor would go to the hospital during their free time to see a patient who's no longer their patient."

"I guess."

"You do know there was nothing more you could have done for Brooke, right?"

Graham's pulse stuttered.

"Everyone worked so hard to save her. Including you. You did everything you could." His gaze held Graham's. "I've just felt lately like I needed to tell you that."

Tears formed at the backs of Graham's eyes, but he fought them and won.

"You loved her well, Graham. It's okay to move on."

"I want to, but—" He shrugged. First he had to figure out how to accomplish that.

"And when—" his dad paused, a small smile creasing his mouth "—or *if* you talk to the Wellings, you do have a secret weapon. A God who moves mountains and changes hearts. Even hardened ones. Mom and I have been praying over your relationship with Lucy ever since you met her."

Graham rubbed a hand over his chest, heart thudding under his fingertips.

"Your mom had a feeling Lucy was the next one for you." Dad grinned. "And this time I agreed with her. So just…don't give up yet."

Suddenly Graham was incredibly grateful for his mother's intuition. Emotion gripped him again, and he cleared his throat before speaking. "Thanks, Dad. I'd better go."

"If you need to stay out and take care of some other things…" His dad went back to doing dishes. "Go right ahead. Mattie will be just fine."

An hour later, Graham stepped into the hospital hallway after finishing his visit with Bill and his family. Bill had started seeing a nephrologist to treat his kidney disease months ago, yet for whatever reason, he always wanted to discuss his treatment options with Graham.

And Graham was learning to accept that.

His thoughts ricocheted as he walked. He was alone. He could go talk to…anyone he wanted to talk to. Like a certain person he'd missed so much this week that a constant ache had weighed down his body, making him wonder if he was sick. He'd finally realized his symptoms were simply from missing Lucy.

Having Hollie back from maternity leave was great. No one did the job quite like her. But Graham wasn't sure he could go another day, another hour without seeing Lucy. Even if she just yelled at him or slapped him, it would be worth it to catch a glimpse of her.

As he walked by the coffee machine, Graham heard his name. He turned to see Olivia.

"Hey." She approached, blowing into a paper coffee cup. "Cash is just in the restroom and then we're headed back in to see her."

His head tilted, brow pinched. "Headed in to see…who?"

The way Olivia's expression went from surprise to concern would have been comical if it didn't tighten something in Graham's gut.

"You're not here to see Lucy?"

Pinpricks raced across his skin as he took a step toward her. "What?"

"Lucy's in the ER." Olivia reached out, putting a hand on his arm for a second as if to calm him. The move didn't work. "I thought maybe she'd let you know."

"No." He struggled for oxygen. "She didn't. Your sister's not exactly the kind to tell anyone when she's hurt or in trouble." Especially him.

She laughed. "So true."

Strange time to be acting so happy. The panic thrumming through him must have been visible on his face, because Olivia squeezed his arm again. "She's okay, Graham."

She couldn't be that okay if she was in the ER. "What's wrong? What happened?"

"She had an allergic reaction."

Before the words were fully spoken, he was headed for the ER.

"Don't you dare break her heart again, Graham Redmond! I'll send Cash after you if you do!"

Graham turned back, the overwhelming need to see Lucy only slightly outweighed by the desire to clarify Olivia's allegiance. If he didn't have her support, he didn't stand a chance with Lucy.

"You aren't going to tell her to run as far from me as she can get? She listens to you and cares what you think. You must want to throttle me for hurting her."

"I did." Olivia's shoulders lifted. "But you'll be relieved to know I'm all about second chances. I have a God and a husband who did the same for me." She made a shooing motion with her hand. "Now get out of here already. It's going to take everything you've got to win her back."

Graham didn't doubt her for a second.

Moments later, he burst into the ER, scanning for someone to help him. When he didn't find anyone, he started peeking into treatment rooms. He could always play his doctor card if someone caught him.

A mess of blond curls spread on a pillow made him stop.

He slowly edged inside. Lucy was lying still, eyes closed, her breathing steady. He attempted to follow suit.

She smelled like summer and lime and everything he never knew he needed.

He studied her skin. Her color looked good. At this point, they were probably watching for a recurrence of her symptoms.

The doctor part of Graham knew she should be fine. But the other part of him—the part that couldn't imagine his life without the woman tucked under a blanket who'd just started snoring like a three-hundred-pound man with sleep apnea—wanted reassurances.

He wanted promises.

But Graham knew better than anyone that life didn't

work that way. He stood by her bed for a number of minutes and watched her sleep, wishing he could wake her with a kiss. Wondering how she'd react if he did.

I love you. The thought seeped into him slowly, warming him. He loved her. He wasn't giving her up.

Which meant right now there was something he had to do…and unfortunately it wasn't watching Lucy sleep. But in the future, if this next conversation went well, that was a job Graham definitely wanted to apply for.

Chapter Eighteen

"I haven't been honest with the two of you." Graham was sitting in the Wellings' living room, and the couple had their rapt attention on him. He'd never been so nervous in all of his life. It felt as though everything depended on this moment, on his ability to convince them to accept Lucy.

He took a calming breath, experiencing a rush of peace when he remembered what his dad had said. His parents were praying. Graham wasn't fighting this battle on his own.

"I wasn't even honest with myself about my feelings. I never thought I'd want to remarry. I had a great marriage with Brooke, and I didn't think that could happen twice. I was content with what I'd had and with being a dad to Mattie. But then Lucy came along." Graham begged for guidance from God, knowing his next words would wound. "I really didn't mean to fall in love with her. That wasn't the plan. But I did. And so did Mattie."

Silence reigned. Belinda wiped a tear with her fingertip.

"I'm willing to give you back Mattie's money if it helps. That's not what Lucy wants. She doesn't even know that money exists, nor would she care. She might come off young and a bit impetuous, and yes, she's not like Brooke, but then… Brooke was one of a kind. And so is Lucy. I'm not trying to steal your memories of Brooke from you. I don't want to hurt you. And I don't want Mattie to lose you from her life because I want to have a relationship with Lucy."

Emotion clogged his throat. "Please don't make me choose between you and Lucy. Mattie needs all of you in her life."

Belinda snagged a tissue, wiping a now steady stream of tears. "It hurts that you would choose her over us. It feels like losing Brooke all over again."

Graham got up and moved next to his mother-in-law on the couch. "I don't want to choose. I want all of you in Mattie's life and my life. I ache for you as parents. I can't imagine losing Mattie. Part of the reason I didn't say anything about Lucy to you earlier is because I didn't want to hurt you. I'm so sorry. I just can't keep burying these feelings."

When Belinda's hand snaked out slowly to squeeze his, the smallest bit of hope sparked.

"So." Phillip shifted in his wingback chair, the same pain on Belinda's face etched on his. "If you and this Lucy have a relationship, you'd still want us in Mattie's life?"

"Of course. I never considered otherwise. I just thought you disliked Lucy so much that you wouldn't be in our lives if I remarried."

"We don't really know Lucy." Belinda looked at her husband. "And we just… We were worried that another woman might come in and steal you and Mattie away from us." Her sob broke him. "And the two of you are all we have left."

"You'll always have us. Nothing is going to change that. And once you get to know Lucy, you'll realize she would never think that way. You're Mattie's grandparents. I don't ever want you to feel shut out of her life. In fact, maybe we can start a better schedule for you with Mattie. A sleepover once a month or something so you're seeing her consistently."

She sniffed. "A date night for you and Lucy."

Graham sighed. He'd thought they were getting some-where.

"I didn't mean that how it sounded." Belinda squeezed his hand again as if the action could communicate what she couldn't. "I meant, it would be nice for you to have the time with Lucy, especially if she's walking right into a family instead of starting one on her own."

That was the closest thing to acceptance Graham had ever heard. Definitely not the response he'd feared or ex-pected. His dad was right. Prayer worked. Without it, this conversation wouldn't be happening.

"We don't want the money back." Phillip leaned forward. "We gave it to you to do as you both saw fit, and we don't need to know what happens to it. If it's going to Mattie's college, that's great. But—" he shook his head "—I, for one, never need to talk about the money again."

Graham nodded. "Okay. One more thing." Phillip and Belinda both tensed. "I'm sorry I never joined the board for Brooke's charity. I'm willing, if you still want me."

"Really?" Both of them looked at him wide-eyed.

"I want another connection, another way to prove to you that inviting Lucy into our lives doesn't mean you're going to lose Mattie."

"Or you." Belinda's mouth gave in to a slight curve. The first smile Graham had seen from either of them since he'd walked through the door.

"Or me."

"Of course we want you on the board." Concern wrin-kled Belinda's brow. "But, Graham, what about this Lucy? Will she ever be able to forgive us? We were horrible to her. We were just hurting so much seeing you move on."

"I think she'll understand and forgive you. She's pretty great that way." The assurance was partly for them, partly for him. If she didn't, he was going to be a huge mess. "But, Belinda?"

"Yes?"

"I think the first step toward mending your relationship with Lucy is to stop putting *this* in front of her name."

"They think it was the mango in the sherbet." Lucy sat in her hospital bed, holding court with Cash and Olivia in the visitor chairs.

Lucy might be a proponent of doing things on her own, but she was going to have to adjust that opinion once again. Everyone should have a sidekick that could fly through traffic fast enough to save their life.

"No mango ever again. It was freaky." Liv wiped a tear. "On the way to the hospital you got so quiet." When Olivia sniffled again and more moisture rolled down her cheeks, Cash pulled a handkerchief from his pocket and offered it to her. For some reason this made her laugh through her tears. "I thought I was going to lose you. I didn't know what to do. Pull over and call an ambulance? Keep driving?"

Cash wrapped an arm around Olivia, pressing a kiss to the top of her head. "I'm thankful you're both okay since I'm sure you weren't exactly obeying traffic laws."

"For reals, McCowboy. What would you do without a wonderful sister-in-law like me? Your life would be incomplete."

The comment earned a grin from him and a groan from her sister.

"You're definitely feeling better."

"I am, especially since I slept a bit."

"Speaking of sleeping, did you have any visitors while we were getting coffee?"

Lucy ignored the pang of disappointment. It wasn't as if she'd sent the text she'd written on her phone earlier.

I need you shouldn't have to be said twice.

"Nope. No visitors."

Olivia and Cash shared a look Lucy couldn't decipher. "Give it time, Liv." Lucy didn't understand Cash's comment, but she let it slide.

"What are you two still doing here anyway?" She made a shooing motion. "It's late. You don't need to wait for me."

"We can stay," Olivia protested.

"Absolutely not."

"What happens when they discharge you?"

"Leave me a set of keys. I feel fine and I can drive myself home."

Cash shrugged. "We do have two vehicles here." He stood and tugged Olivia up with him. "Come on. Lucy's right. She's fine. You heard it straight from the doctor. And I'm guessing you're about as emotionally exhausted right now as can be."

Olivia covered a yawn. "Not true. I'm a rock."

"Yep. You are." He grinned, and the way he looked at her sister made Lucy fight a rush of emotion.

"Okay, enough sap, you two. Have you forgotten I recently had my heart broken? Get out of here before you mess me up again."

They came over and gave her hugs, and once they'd gone, Lucy snuggled under the light blanket on her bed. For a moment earlier, when she'd woken up, she'd been positive that she could smell Graham. That he'd been here.

Maybe the medicine had messed with her mind.

Now Lucy felt completely fine and wanted to get out of the hospital. But since the ER moved at a snail's pace, she assumed she had a wait on her hands.

"Did someone order a doctor?" Graham peeked into her room.

"Hey." Lucy sat up against her pillows. Those mad-at-him/please-kiss-me feelings came rushing back. "What are you doing here?"

"Technically, I am your doctor."

"No, you're not."

"You worked in my office, Lucy. I think that counts as close enough to a patient."

Oh. How disappointing. He'd come to see her because

he was Graham and he was noble. He was right to come, though, because they had to learn to be friends again and function around each other. Especially if Lucy planned to stay in this town.

And due to the news she'd found out this week—that the owner of the dance school she worked at wanted to sell the business within the next few years—that possibility was getting more and more definite.

Lucy could do this. She could get through a conversation with Graham. Then the next one *had* to be easier.

"I know I'm not exactly your favorite person right now, but I figured these were extenuating circumstances." Instead of sitting in a chair, he perched on the edge of her bed. Her pulse started drumming like crazy at his close proximity and the fact that she hadn't inhaled him in almost a week.

When his hand found hers and held on, the machine monitoring Lucy's heart betrayed her, broadcasting her body's reaction to his touch.

"How are you feeling?"

"Much better."

"I'm glad to hear that." His hand switched from cradling hers to entwining fingers. "Lucy, I love you."

Her mouth slacked open and her throat closed off again. A rush of goose bumps spread across her skin, but she tamped down any excitement at hearing those words from him.

Love wasn't enough.

Not with how the Wellings felt about her, and Graham bargaining over her.

"Phillip and Belinda are going to apologize to you. They were upset about me moving on because it made them feel like they were losing Brooke all over again. They thought us being in a relationship would take me and Mattie away from them."

Indignation straightened her spine. "I would never do that."

"I know. That's what I told them."

"And they…accepted that?"

He nodded slowly, and something close to hope started flapping wings in her chest. Lucy shoved it down again. He'd hurt her. How could she just forget about that?

"Lucy, I'm sorry I made a deal with the Wellings and didn't tell you what was really going on. I was so busy denying my feelings for you I didn't even realize what I'd done." He tucked a piece of her hair behind her ear, fingers lingering against her cheek and wreaking havoc on her emotions. "Until it was too late."

It's not too late.

Yes, it is.

The thoughts warred as Liv's advice came rushing back. *Forgive him.*

Lucy could have everything she wanted. Or none of it.

Graham's hold on her hand loosened, his shoulders wearing the same hurt she felt coursing through her. Was he going to leave?

Panic rose up, screaming for attention. How could she even consider letting him go? She might not want to need anyone, but she needed this man.

"You hurt me, Hollywood."

Regret clung to his features. "I know. And I'm so sorry. I never want you to feel like that again. The things that make you *you* are exactly what I love about you. I'll do anything I can to make it up to you. To prove how I really feel about you."

Anything.

Ideas started forming.

"Like another road trip? That purse I wanted?"

His low chuckle warmed her from the toes up, and the heart monitor started giving away her every emotion again.

"Can you turn that thing off?"

Graham did something to the machine and the screen went blank.

"That was so not like you, breaking rules, turning things off that are supposed to be on."

He just grinned and sat back on the edge of the bed. "I won't do anything to mess with you being okay. I kind of have a thing for you."

"You do?"

"Yep. And I wonder if you noticed I said I love you." His head tilted. "I didn't hear a response to that, though I know for certain you said you loved me once before."

"That conversation was a week ago." She tried desperately to keep her lips from curving. "So much has changed since then."

His eyes narrowed. "Still counts as good for me. I'm holding you to it."

"You're awfully demanding." His lips were dropping to hers, and she was having a hard time concentrating on anything else.

"And somehow, even in a hospital bed, you're beautiful." He kissed her.

It was a good thing her heart monitor had been turned off. His kiss was gentle—almost reverent. He memorized her face with his lips, and Lucy fell into the knowledge that something had changed between them. Now, along with the tingling current that always ebbed, there was also a strength. A sense that she was safe. She'd never known before what it felt like to have everything she wanted within reach.

Good night. She couldn't give in that easily. Lucy placed her hands on his chest and pushed, but he gave her only a few inches of space.

"Do you think this is some kind of done deal or something?"

His mouth curved, causing her stomach to tap-dance. "Yep."

"Well, it's not."

"Okay." He stood and started disconnecting wires and cords.

"What are you doing?"

"Getting you out of here."

She clutched the blanket. He couldn't do that, could he?

"By the way, are you in pajamas?"

"Yeah. I was wearing them when the reaction happened."

"Why?"

"I was wallowing."

His brow furrowed. "I'm sorry if you were wallowing because of me. I'm sorry I didn't talk to the Wellings earlier, that I didn't fight for you. For us. Although, I'm not sure that conversation would have gone so well without an extreme amount of prayer. I'm still in shock that it did. Isn't it funny how we ask God for something and then we're surprised when He answers us?"

Recognition of that truth settled in her soul. "I do that all the time." This. This was why she needed to ask God to handle things instead of trying to do everything on her own. She'd wanted this, but God had made this happen. Not her. She'd always thought she had to do everything on her own. But when that got stripped away from her, she'd found the God she'd been missing. The one who didn't need her to be in charge. The one who, turned out, already had everything under control.

Graham continued to mess with all of the stuff connected to her. Removed her IV.

"Don't I need that?"

"Nope. You're not even getting medicine through it anymore."

"Then why am I here?"

"You won't be for long."

Suddenly she was being lifted from the bed. Graham was cradling her, carrying her out of the ER.

"Tight security around here. I'm being abducted and no one even blinks."

"I don't think anyone would be upset to find out your future husband—who's a doctor—is taking you. Plus..." His grin turned sheepish. "I checked with the doctor before I came in to see you and got all of your paperwork. You're fine. And I already got you an EpiPen."

Of course he had.

Did he just say *future husband*?

Giddiness threaded through her. "Who says I'm marrying you?"

"I do."

Her arms were wrapped around his neck, and Lucy had to admit, she was enjoying the ride. "You'd better check your sources. Last I heard, a man usually asks a woman to marry him. He doesn't demand it caveman style. What makes you think I'm going to marry you, anyway?"

"This." He slid her down until her feet touched the ground, one hand holding her against him, one wrapped into her hair. He kissed her until she could hardly stand before pulling back. "And the fact that I love you and you love me, and when you're done being snarky, you're going to admit it."

"Oh." Her voice was as wobbly as her legs. She slipped her hands behind his neck, pulling him down for another kiss. "I do love you. You're easy to love."

Too soon, he inched back again, sliding his hands to her shoulders. His evergreen eyes were filled with so much love she considered heading back to her hospital bed for a hit of oxygen.

"Lucy, will you marry me and Mattie? We have this big hole that only you can fill. We need you."

Her stupid eyes were leaking. "I knew you were for me. I just didn't know if I was going to get to keep you."

"Keep me. Please. I'm a mess without you."

"Yes." She touched his face, wondering over the fact that

she was being proposed to in a hospital hallway and she couldn't envision a more romantic scenario. "I'd wanted to fix this. To make sure the Wellings' relationship was back on track with Mattie. But you and God fixed it instead of me."

"God gets all the credit. There's no other explanation for how that conversation went so well." His hands slid down her arms, warmth seeping through her long-sleeved T-shirt. "And I thought I had to save everyone, that everything rested on my shoulders. But then you came along and saved me and Mattie when we didn't even know we needed it."

"My heart is beating all wild again."

He scooped her back into his arms. "It's because you love me. But just to be safe, I'd better carry you out of here."

Lucy looked up at the man she wanted for forever and let go of a contented sigh.

Being rescued wasn't such a bad thing after all.

Epilogue

Three weeks later, Lucy met Graham and Mattie at the bottom of her apartment steps. Since little eyes were watching, Lucy's first instinct—jumping into Graham's arms—was a no go. Instead, she settled for a nice long hug from each of them.

"So, Mattie Grace, where are we going?"

Mattie shook her head, eyes sparkling behind her red glasses. "Dad says we can't tell."

Graham held out his hand. "I need your car keys."

"What? Why?"

"Because my car is washed, and yours isn't."

"I think I'm offended, but I'll forgive you if you tell me where we're going."

His mouth curved. "Duchess, I already told you—you're on a need-to-know basis."

"But I need to know!"

He put his hands on her shoulders and directed her to the passenger seat of her car. "Get in. We have to do something." He started backing out of her door, then popped back in to place a kiss on her cheek. "Close your eyes." His whisper made her skin tingle.

"Fine." She complied, unable to keep the smile from her face. Graham had told her casual—that was all she knew—

so she'd paired black skinny jeans with a flowy white shirt and pink Chucks. She heard the trunk open and a bunch of scrambling, some finagling of what she assumed was a car seat going into the back. After a minute, the car door shut.

"Okay, you can open them now." Graham grinned at Mattie in the rearview mirror and started the car. The two of them were dressed casually, like her—Mattie in a yellow sundress and boots, and Graham in jeans and a button-up shirt. Lucy's curiosity hovered near boiling. Where could they be headed?

He drove out of town, and she somehow resisted asking questions. Finally, they reached a turnoff. Gorgeous bluebonnets stretched before them, and white and yellow flowers also speckled the roadside and fields. Lucy agreed with Mattie's excitement coming from the backseat. It was unlike anything she'd ever seen before.

"This is a good surprise." She shared a smile with Graham.

"It's going to get—"

"Hey!" Graham cut off Mattie's next words, and she giggled from the backseat.

After a few minutes driving slowly along with other cars looking at the wildflowers, Graham signaled and turned onto a small dirt road, driving the car around a patch of trees and then parking.

"This doesn't look like a well-worn path. Are we trespassing or something?" So not something Graham would do, but none of the other cars had turned.

Graham laughed. "We're good. I have my sources. And patients."

"And your patients let you tromp around on their land?"

"Yep. Come on." He hopped out, and Lucy followed him and a bouncing Mattie to the trunk. They opened it, revealing a picnic spread. A brown basket brimming with fruit, cheese, meat and crackers. A cooler filled with drinks. Graham grabbed a plaid blanket and spread it out, the amazing flowers a backdrop all around them.

In the past three weeks, Graham and Lucy had gone on a few dates by themselves, and although those dates had been nice—okay, they'd been wonderful and Olivia had been teasing Lucy about walking around wearing a silly grin—this one was equally great in a whole different way. This felt like a glimpse of what was to come. In between bites of food, Mattie ran around in the field, looking like a wild flower child. She'd blossomed so much in a short amount of time. It was as if she finally knew she was safe—that all of her people were getting along.

Lucy had also made progress with the Wellings over the past few weeks. Their interactions weren't perfect, but they were all making an effort. And Lucy knew the chance to be with Graham and Mattie was worth the extra work she would continue to put forth with the couple.

After they ate, Graham stood and held out his hand to her. "Should we take a walk?"

"Sure." They took the dirt path—only two tire tracks cutting through the field popping with color.

"I have something to show you." Graham twined his fingers with hers, touching the gorgeous engagement ring he'd given her a few days after proposing at the hospital. She'd always known the man had good taste.

They rounded the bend and a beautiful dark wood barn came into view. What was going on?

Mattie ran up ahead, then came flying back to them, excitement evident.

Graham squeezed Lucy's hand. "So, what do you think?"

She scanned the landscape. A gorgeous barn in the middle of a field of wildflowers. She didn't quite know how to answer his question.

"It's beautiful."

"It's being remodeled into a place to hold weddings." *Oh.* Now she liked it even better.

"I've seen the plans for the inside, and it's going to be amazing. I'll show them to you and then you can decide."

"I'd like to see them, but I already know I love it."

"Are you sure? I know wedding stuff is a big deal."

"I pretty much just want to have a huge party and invite everyone I know."

"Why am I not surprised?" A grin claimed his mouth. "We could be the first wedding here."

"Patient-doctor privilege?"

He nodded.

"Where do we sign up?"

Mattie clapped and spun in circles. "We're going to get married here, and I'm going to have a white dress. Then you'll be ours, Lucy. Daddy told me that's how a wedding works."

She scooped Mattie into a hug, meeting Graham's gaze over the top of her head. "I'm already yours." The smile that met hers warmed her from the inside out. "Cover your eyes, Mattie Grace."

"Why?"

"Because I want to kiss your dad."

"Eww!" Mattie shoved her hands over her eyes, and Lucy leaned into Graham.

"It's a good thing you asked me to marry you."

Humor tugged on his lips. "Oh, yeah? Why's that?"

"Because I kind of have a thing for you two." She kissed him, though not for as long as she would have liked. There would be plenty of time for those kisses in the days, weeks and years to come. She peppered Mattie's cheeks with smooches, and Graham joined in. The girl screamed and tried to squirm away from them, giggling with a belly laugh that made Lucy's heart go gooey.

The Mattie effect was still in full force.

When Lucy let go, Mattie dropped to the ground and ran ahead, still yelling and laughing as if she was being chased.

Graham tugged Lucy against his chest, and she slid her

arms around his waist. When Mattie disappeared around the bend in front of them, his lips found the sensitive spot just under her ear. Turned out that whole patience thing wasn't really her gig. "I think finding the perfect place to have our wedding deserves a real kiss. Am I right?"

Strong arms tightened around her, his curved mouth hovering over hers. "Always."

* * * * *

Dear Reader,

I hope you enjoyed Graham and Lucy's story as much as I enjoyed writing it.

Many years ago I moved to live with my sister in Colorado. I didn't think of that as the catalyst for this book, but now I wonder if that's where the idea sprouted from. I only knew once Lucy appeared in *Falling for Texas* she simply *had* to have her own book. I love the difference between Graham's and Lucy's personalities and how they end up complementing each other. In my opinion, they were the perfect mismatch. Thanks for giving me the opportunity to write about them!

Like Lucy, I often fail at asking for help. I fall into the trap of attempting to fix everything on my own before realizing, once again, that God's solution is so much better than mine. I've seen beautiful things come from relationships where people are strong enough to ask for help. I'm a work in progress in this area, thankful for a heavenly Father who loves each of us just as we are.

I love to connect with readers. Find me on Facebook, Twitter, Instagram and Pinterest, and at Jill-Lynn.com. And if you enjoyed *Her Texas Family* and would consider writing a quick review, I'd be very grateful.

Blessings,
Jill Lynn

When Kayla had discovered she had a bodyguard, she hadn't expected this. He should be in the background, quietly observing. Her father was a lawyer and a politician; she'd seen bodyguards and knew how they did their jobs. And yet here she sat with this family, her bodyguard talking of cattle and fixing fence as his sisters tried to cajole him into taking them to look at a pair of horses owned by Kayla's brother.

A hand settled on her back. She glanced at the man next to her, his dark eyes crinkled at the corners and his mouth quirked, revealing a dimple in his left cheek.

Boone opened his mouth as if to say something but a heavy knock on the front door interrupted. He pushed away from the table and gave them all an apologetic look.

"I think I'll get that." His gaze landed on Kayla. "You stay right where you are until I say otherwise."

"They wouldn't come here," she said. And she'd meant to sound strong; instead it came out like a question.

"We don't know what they would or wouldn't do, because we don't know who they are. Stay." Boone walked away, his brother Jase getting up and going after him.

Kayla avoided looking at his family, who still remained at the table. Conversation had of course ended. She knew they were looking at her. She knew that she had invaded their life.

And she knew that her bodyguard might seem like a relaxed cowboy, but he wasn't. He was the man standing between her and the unknown.

Don't miss
HER RANCHER BODYGUARD
by Brenda Minton, available June 2016 wherever
Love Inspired® books and ebooks are sold.

www.LoveInspired.com

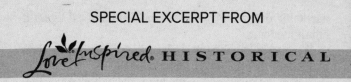
"Make another move, and I'll shoot you where you
stand..." He trailed off, jaw sagging. Had he entered the
wrong house?

"Don't shoot! I can explain! I—I have a letter. From
Will Canfield." A petite dark-haired woman standing on the
other side of his table lifted an envelope in silent entreaty.

At the mention of his friend's name, he slowly lowered
his weapon. But his defensive instincts still surged
through him. When he didn't speak, she gestured limply
to the ornate leather trunks stacked on either side of his
bedroom door. "Mr. Canfield was supposed to meet us at
the station. His porter arrived in his stead... Simon was
his name. He said something about a posse and outlaws."
A delicate shudder shook her frame. "He said you
wouldn't mind if we brought these inside. I do apologize
for invading your home like this, but I had no idea when
you would return, and it is June out there."

Her gaze roamed his face, her light brown eyes
widening ever so slightly as they encountered his scars.
It was like this every time. He braced himself for the

inevitable disgust. Pity. Revulsion. Told himself again it didn't matter.

When her expression reflected nothing more than curiosity, irrational anger flooded him.

"What are you doing in my home?" he snapped. "How do you know Will?"

"I'm Constance Miller. I'm the bride Mr. Canfield sent for."

"Will's already got a wife."

Pink kissed her cheekbones. "Not for him. For you."

His throat closed. He wouldn't have.

"I was summoned to Cowboy Creek to be your bride. Your friend didn't tell you." A sharp crease brought her brows together.

"I'm afraid not." Slipping off his worn Stetson, Noah hooked it on the chair and dipped his head toward the crumpled parchment. "May I?"

Miss Miller didn't appear inclined to approach him, so he laid his gun on the mantel and crossed to the square table. He took the envelope she extended across to him and slipped the letter free. The handwriting was unmistakable. Heat climbed up his neck as he read the description of himself. He stuffed it back inside and tossed it onto the tabletop. "I'm afraid you've come all the way out here for nothing. The trip was a waste, Miss Miller. I am not, nor will I ever be, in the market for a bride."

Don't miss
BRIDE BY ARRANGEMENT
by Karen Kirst, available June 2016 wherever
Love Inspired® Historical books and ebooks are sold.

www.LoveInspired.com